NOTES FROM THE
GUTS OF A HIPPO

Grant Wamack

Bizarro Pulp Press
www.BIZARROPULPPRESS.com
Notes from the Guts of a Hippo Copyright © 2013
Grant Wamack

ISBN-13:978-0615765228
ISBN-10: 061576522X

Printed in the USA.

THE NOVELLA DEDICATED TO ALL OF THE
JOURNALISTS AND JOURNALISTAS OF THE WORLD.

GRANT WAMACK

1

The cell phone rang.

Once.

Twice.

On the third ring, Jay Robbins answered it. "Hello?"

A smooth voice answered, "Yeah, it's me . . . Ron." He paused, as if testing the waters. "Jay, I need you to come back. I'm sorry about the whole fiasco with the pandas and the balloons. Things didn't go exactly as planned."

Jay sat in darkness on his bed rubbing his free hand through his hair. He considered hanging up, something inside told him not to. Maybe it was his empty pockets or the gnawing hunger in his gut. "What's the job, Ron? A shooting? A hostage situation?"

"No, no, it's a little off the beaten path. Once I received the info I thought you would be the perfect fit. Have you ever heard of Patrick Little?" the smooth voice asked.

The name sounded vaguely familiar. "No, I've been busy. I haven't had a chance to watch the tube. Who is he?" Jay replied.

"He's the foremost expert in the field of hippopotamus research. Rumor has it he was last seen in Brazil searching for a rare breed of hippo, the legendary Lastiz. Then one day, out of the blue, he disappeared. One of his assistants wandered inside his tent and found nothing but a dirty sock. They combed the surrounding area for any traces of him but came up empty handed."

"So you need me to go to Brazil to find this . . . hippo researcher?" Jay wiped the drool from his mouth.

"Yes, and I want you to bring back a story for the paper as well. You don't have to worry about anything. We will supply you with everything you need once you reach Brazil."

"Okay," he said reluctantly.

2

Jay packed a small black, battered suitcase, turned off the lights, locked his doors, and went outside. A yellow cab idled by the curb. Grudgingly, he slipped inside and set his suitcase on the seat next to him.

It was a little stuffy so Jay unbuttoned his shirt a few notches. When he looked up, he saw the cab driver staring at him in the rearview mirror. "Uh . . . hi there." He fixed his eyes on the back of the cab driver's shiny bald head. It was shaped like an oversized egg.

Keeping his back turned, the cab driver spoke in a heavy Italian accent, "Hi. I drive you."

Before Jay could even make sense of what those words entailed, the cab driver slammed his foot on the pedal. He sat in absolute terror, clutching the back of the passenger seat as the car made a sharp turn. The tires screeched loudly. That's when he noticed the man's head swaying slightly to the right. Any more momentum and his head might crash through the passenger side window.

Worried, Jay licked his chapped lips.

"Don't you think we should slow down?" he asked, fear tugging at the edge of his voice.

The driver turned around and his head began to lean dangerously to the left. Jay became disturbed when he saw the driver had no face whatsoever, just a shiny surface with a slit for mouth. That's when an eighteen wheeler came out of nowhere, smashing the small cab into a red brick warehouse.

Fade to black.

3

Jay woke, absentmindedly feeling the knots on his head. His mouth tasted strange, bitter. A moment later, he recognized the coppery taste for what it was.

Blood.

Jay looked around. The cab was a complete wreck, its insides spilled out into the intersection. Smoke curled into the air trying to touch the sky. A few misshapen bodies littered the ground. He felt a sharp pain shoot up his right leg.

Goddamn it. He rubbed his leg.

Somewhere in the distance an engine revved. He looked around for the source but couldn't find it anywhere.

The cab driver slowly stood, inspecting himself for any injuries. An eighteen wheeler flew into his path out of nowhere. He ran as fast as he could, speed didn't prove to be one of his gifts.

An old man stuck his head out the window and laughed loudly. He coughed and something fell out his mouth, clattering on the ground.

Terrified, Jay hurried over to the cab driver. There was a large dent on the right side of his head and blood began dribbling out of his head onto the deserted street.

A shroud of guilt weighed on his thoughts. *I messed up*, he thought. *This is all my fault.* Then he noticed something yellow amid the blood.

Jay reached out and grabbed the object.

"Shit," he said in disgust.

He immediately dropped it, recognizing it for what it was. Yellowed dentures.

Jay thought about leaving and calling it quits there and then, but he desperately needed the cash. The human instinct for survival overrode the mixture of guilt and disgust that bubbled deep inside his gut.

Sirens screamed in the distance.

Wasting no time, Jay stuffed the bloody dentures into the back pocket of his jeans. He spotted a beat up Chevy Civic the color of green vomit. He ran over and busted the window with his good foot. Before jumping in, he cleaned off the shards of glass from the driver's seat. He ducked underneath the steering wheel, dug around, and found two wires. He put the wires tips together and the car sparked to life.

Jay sped away in a cold sweat.

4

Jay sat in first class on a jetliner headed toward the heart of Brazil. *This is what I call comfort*, he thought, downing his third shot of vodka. He felt a little tipsy. The rest of the trip was spent in a drunken stupor.

The jet eased into the airport after an uneventful flight. Jay stumbled across the gate with a throbbing headache and sweaty palms.

"Damn, it's hot," he muttered.

A tall, skinny man wearing cheap sunglasses ran around asking every male if his name was Jay. Jay tried to hurry past—keeping his head low—but the tall man saw everything under the sun, including Jay. He ran up and grabbed Jay's collar.

Jay smacked the man's large hand down as if it were a fly.

"Hey! You're Jay, aren't you?" The tall man held his hand and looked pained. "That was very rude."

"I'm not in the mood."

"Ron told me you would say that." The tall man picked up his pace to keep up with Jay as he speed walked, hands and legs pumping furiously.

"Look, Jay, my name is Eric Liboot. Ron paid me to be your personal guide. I'm supposed to help you stay out of trouble."

"Well I don't need any help with that, trouble seems to follow me everywhere I go."

"That's exactly why I should be your guide," Eric reasoned.

"Whatever. Just keep your mouth shut and try not to get in my way," Jay said, moodily. He didn't need a babysitter. He was a grown man, dammit.

5

Jay and Eric walked down street in need of some lunch.

They arrived at a joint named Raving Ramone's. A few people sat outside, chowing down on some food. There was no door, just an arched entranceway with multi-colored stringed beads hanging down. As Jay walked inside he wondered how they prevented thieves and bums from overrunning the place.

"The world's going to hell, I'm telling ya. You need proof? Just turn on the TV and you will see. Lemons, apples, and peaches, but what about the bananas? Does anyone care about the bananas?" Ramone's bloodshot eyes seemed ready to burst out the sockets.

He was a large, muscular man with long dirty dreadlocks who busily surveyed the room for any answers. Everyone kept their mouth shut; a few people left intimidated.

"Just peel back the layers," Ramone muttered before returning to a darkly lit corner.

"So let me guess, that would be Ramone?" Jay asked.

"Yeah. Ramone lost a few screws a while back. Long story," Eric said.

"Damn. That's sad," Jay said.

"Don't feel sorry for him. The ladies love him. Maybe they feel sorry for the guy. Or maybe they just like the way he looks. Either way he's swimming in pussy. Just look over there," Eric gestured.

Jay looked in the direction he pointed. Two tanned beauties cuddled tightly against Ramone. One was a dirty blonde who giggled constantly while the other, a brunette, nodded at every word that came out of Ramone's lips.

"Well, it sure looks that way. Lucky bastard," Jay said.

The waiter walked up to the table. He sported a crew cut and an immaculate black suit. He was sweating like a fat man yet he seemed fit as fit can be.

"Hi, what can I do for you guys? Can I start you off with something to drink, maybe some appetizers?" he asked, notepad in hand, pencil raised and ready.

Eric glanced at the menu and then looked at Jay. "What do you want?"

"Let's get some appetizers. How about some jerk chicken wings? We could split them," Jay reasoned.

"Yeah. That's fine with me," Eric said.

The waiter came back in a jiffy with the drinks. Jay had a Pepsi and Eric an ice tea. Both thanked the waiter before he turned to another table of customers.

A man dressed in raggedy clothes ran into the

restaurant. Frantic, he scanned the room. Then his eyes stopped, finally resting on Jay and Eric.

"Oh, god. Here comes another bozo." Eric spoke a little too loud for comfort.

The raggedy man ran over and dropped to his hands and knees and crawled underneath the table. Eric turned to Jay. Jay looked elsewhere as if nothing had happened.

"Jay?" Eric's forehead creased in worry.

Jay said nothing, whistling a little tune instead.

"Jay, we can't ignore the guy. He's right under the table. What are we gonna do? Just act as if there's nobody there?"

"Yes. That's the only way to solve things. If I don't acknowledge his existence, then, *poof*," Jay said, gesturing like magician who just completed a disappearing act. "He will cease to exist."

"Jesus Christ. I can't believe this. At least I'm getting paid. If I wasn't—"

"Your wings are done." The waiter grinned widely and placed the large plate of steaming wings on the middle of the table. "If there's anything else you guys need, don't be afraid to ask."

After the waiter left, Eric said, "I need a gun so I can blow my fuckin brains out. But first, let me eat a few of these wings. A man's got to eat."

Jay wiped the sauce off his face. "That really hit the spot," he said.

"Yeah. I almost forgot how good the cooking is. I mean nothing but quality. Grade fucking A," Eric said.

Jay took his bowl of bones and slid it under

the table.

A moment later, bones crunched noisily.

"Don't feed the thing. I know they're just bones but come on, Jay. Is he paying for any of the food? No, so don't feed him unless you intend to bring him home."

"Be careful. I might do it."

"Why did I even take this job?" Eric put his face in his hands.

The raggedy man poked his head out from underneath the table. "Hey . . . uh . . . I need your help."

"Speak your piece," Jay said.

"*They're* after me. *They're* on my tail. I need to keep my head low, somewhere I can hide." The raggedy man looked paranoid.

"Who exactly are *they*?" Eric asked.

"They're the I.R.S.. I'm wanted for tax evasion."

"Damn. Looks like you're in some deep shit," Eric said.

"Yeah. Very deep. I thought maybe fleeing America would help. But no, no siree. The government follows you wherever you go. You can't shake them. Bunch of crabs I tell ya." The raggedy man nervously scratched his shoulder.

"So what do we get in return for looking over you?" Jay sipped his Pepsi.

"Cold hard cash." The raggedy man dug into his pockets and pulled out a fat wad of 100 dollar bills. "Here. Here. Take it."

Jay took the cash, sniffed it, and stuffed it in his

pocket. Eric looked at the raggedy man with contempt and then glared at Jay.

"This isn't part of the job, Jay." Every word was wrapped in barbwire. "Find the researcher and get the story. That's it. None of this baby-sit the bum bullshit."

"Well, we're doing it. And that's that. Just relax. You'll get your cut."

"Oh, shit! There are two of them at the entrance!" The raggedy man ducked back underneath the table.

Two men dressed in black suits, sporting stylish black shades, stood at the entranceway surveying the restaurant from left to right. They began walking around, looking everyone up and down. One even went insofar as to sniff the air as if he could catch the unique scent of the raggedy man.

After what felt like an eternity, the men left and took a complimentary loaf of bread with them. Everyone took one large breath of relief.

"That was a close one," Eric said.

"You have no idea." The raggedy man looked up at him, eyes pleading.

"I think we should take our leave. Where's the check?" Jay said. Once the waiter was in sight, he waved him over.

A few minutes passed, the waiter came back with the check in hand. Eric paid and everyone chipped in for the tip, including the raggedy man.

They walked down the street, just the three of them. Jay, Eric, and the raggedy man in between. The raggedy man looked around constantly for the men in black. Despite his best efforts to stay calm and blend in, he stuck out like a sore thumb.

"Relax. Keep a level head." Jay patted the raggedy man's back.

"All right, all right." The raggedy man tried to relax by breathing in his nose and out his mouth.

"What are you going to say, Jay? Way to be a trooper?"

Jay just ignored him, which only infuriated Eric more.

After a few blocks of tension plus a river's worth of sweat, they found a Motel 8. Thick vines creeped over half the building like green veins. Even with the ugly brickwork it looked like a paradise.

Inside the spacious lobby, an old man leaned against the counter fanning himself with a magazine. Jay watched his movements closely, looking for anything that might match him with the driver of the large semi-truck back in the states.

When he turned around and smiled, all of Jay's worries turned to dust. He realized his face wasn't right; it was far too angular. And to top it off, this man still had his own teeth, despite their yellowness.

The hotel manager came up to the counter. He had a grimy nametag pinned to his blue velvet jacket that read Steve. Sweat stains covered his white undershirt.

"All right sir, just sign here please," Steve said.

The old man signed.

"And if you would be so kind, here."

He signed yet again.

"Now just right here."

He did so, but his hand began to cramp afterward.

"Okay, you're all set. Just leave your bags here. These men will escort you to Hell. Motel 8 now owns your soul." Steve grinned.

The old man looked stunned. The news forced new wrinkles on top of old wrinkles. With his shoulders slumped, he resigned himself to the terms of the contract.

Two men in charred black suits came out, grabbed him by his feet, and dragged the man through a set of double doors which presumably led to Hell. He didn't make a sound.

The raggedy man was on the floor curled into the fetal position, trying his best to squeeze tight inside himself.

"Oh, god! Come on, get up and act like a fuckin' adult! Everyone who wears a black suit isn't out to get you," Eric said.

"I don't know Eric, politicians, lawyers—"

"Okay, okay. You're right, Jay. But regular Joes, the nobodies in black suits aren't out to get you. Believe me."

Cautiously, the raggedy man stretched his body out like petals on a blossoming flower.

Steve came back to the counter. He rubbed his big hands against one another, and the corners of his mouth turned upward into a thin veneer of a smile.

"So what can I do for you?"

"Just need a room for about a week."

"Okay." Steve clattered away on the computer before he said, "We have a room available with two

19

king sized beds. Would this be acceptable?"

"Yes. That would be *acceptable*," Eric replied.

"Okay, if you could just sign here."

Steve handed over a huge stack of papers. Jay carefully read over each page, making sure he didn't miss anything. Today wasn't the day he'd be going to Hell.

Jay signed the papers. Steve took them and disappeared for a moment.

"I hope you read everything. And I mean everything." The raggedy man shifted from toe to toe.

"Do you want to stay with us? I mean, I would have no problem leaving you out there to get torn apart by the dogs. No guilty conscience. Nothing," Jay said.

The raggedy man shook his head quickly and straightened his body out. "No, no, no. I saw you read it. You have twenty-twenty vision, the best two eyes I have ever seen."

"Don't turn sweet on me now," Jay said.

"I'm not."

Steve came back holding a silver key in his hand. It gleamed in the light.

"Room 207." He handed the key over.

Jay took the key and stuffed it into his pocket. They rode the elevator up to the second floor. Incidentally, the room wasn't far, just a few doors down.

The room was also thinly furnished, nothing special about it except the view, which was spectacular. The windows provided a panoramic shot of the mountains, lush with green jungle, and a setting sun.

"The sun is going down. I think it's time to get some shuteye." The raggedy man stretched out his skinny arms.

"Yeah, some sleep would do us all some good," Jay said.

"You guys act like little girls. *Let's get some sleep.* How about we get some hookers and fuck them until our dicks fall off? Who really needs sleep?" Eric gave off waves of excitement.

"Everyone needs sleep. And I don't know about you, but I need my dick."

"Don't fuck with me, Jay. I have had it up to here with you."

"What you gonna do about it Eric, piss yourself?"

Then, Eric began shaking violently and a vein popped out of his forehead. His face changed from a light tan to lobster red in a matter of seconds. Fists clenched, he spontaneously combusted. Flaming slabs of skin and blood smacked against the walls, followed by his organs and bones, which made an even worse racket as they slammed into the furniture.

The raggedy man and Jay stood in absolute shock and awe.

"I'm . . . I'm going to bed." The raggedy man slid into a bed and hid underneath the sheets.

"Uh . . . good idea."

Jay closed the shades and turned out the lights. He glanced over at the dark hump in the bed before slipping into the one beside it.

Jay couldn't sleep. He just stared at the ceiling, tracing the small cracks and indentations with his eyes. When he finally began to drift off, he heard muffled voices in the hall. *Damn, who's outside?* he wondered.

A thick block of silence passed before the door was ripped off its hinges. Two men in black suits walked into the room. They dusted the dirt off their shoulders and adjusted their shades.

Jay quickly rolled off the bed and dropped to all fours. He forced himself not to make a sound. His muscles felt tense, but he forced his body to be silent, alert. *Be one with the floor*, he thought. *One with the floor*.

One of the men bent down and picked up one of Eric's bones. It looked like a femur. However, Jay wasn't one hundred percent sure. The man snapped it in half with his bare hands and began sucking the marrow inside.

"This is some good shit, man," he said to his partner.

"Save some for me." He cocked his gun.

The raggedy man mumbled something, but his words were soon cut off by gunshots fired into his body.

Slowly, Jay pulled himself up to a crouched position. He crept by the men, skirting the edges of the room. By the time he was outside he didn't care how much noise he made. It couldn't be heard over the screams or the pounding of shots through the bed, wall, and flesh.

A non-descript fat man stood in the hallway, scratching his balls, and holding an ice bucket. He headed down the hall, most likely on his way to get some ice.

Jay tried the door handle. It opened into a room that was an exact replica of 207. Everything was the same: the chairs, the painting, the windows. The only thing off was the view. He scanned the room for anything he could use as a weapon. However, nothing seemed to be useful or quiet enough. He settled on the only reliable thing left: his hands.

The fat man came back into the room and yawned as he set the bucket of ice down on a small table. Jay came up behind him, slick with silence. The fat man was about to release a scream, but Jay muffled it with a quick jab to the ribs and covered his mouth with his free hand. The man's hot breath caressed his palm.

"Be quiet."

The fat man tried to speak.

"I said, shut the fuck up. Don't make me repeat myself."

Jay put him in a sleeper hold. He squeezed.

The fat man struggled.

He squeezed even harder, adding more pressure every second.

Soon, the fat man went limp.

"It's time to sleep. My condolences to the Sandman," Jay whispered.

Jay picked up the man, who was surprisingly light, and tucked him into one of the beds. Then he considered slipping into the other bed. Just laying his head on the pillow. *Don't be stupid*, he thought. *You're smarter than that. You wouldn't want to be caught sleeping, would you?*

So instead, he slipped under the bed and waited.

6

Sunlight crept into the room. Eventually, it reached Jay's hand, which curled and uncurled in the throes of a dream.

Jay woke feeling out of place. He moaned as he turned over instinctively reaching out for covers, but found nothing.

After rubbing his eyes, his thoughts drifted from nothingness back to reality. He remembered everything with a striking clarity. The horrible stench of Eric's spontaneous combustion and the raggedy man's screams as the I.R.S. sent him to kingdom come. And finally, he realized he was in someone else's room.

Jay poked his head out from underneath the bed and listened for any sounds. Eventually, he heard the fat man grunt and the springs of the bed screech, barely containing his immense weight.

Jay slipped out and stood to his feet. His body cracked and popped out of stiffness. His throat felt dry, and he had to take a piss.

He walked out the room and softly closed the door. He expected to see men in black suits taping off his room, but oddly enough, everything in the hallway remained the same. He thought about walking down to room 207 and looking inside. But he knew curiosity killed the cat, and it killed a buddy of his a few years back.

The elevator was empty and so was the lobby when Jay entered. He found the men's washroom to be to his liking. Plain and simple, nothing fancy about it. A man could just walk in, unzip his pants, and . . . sweet heaven.

Once outside, he found the wind had a little bit of an edge to it. Still, he didn't mind. It helped him wake up.

He thought about Eric. He tried to avoid it, focusing on the situation at hand, but no matter where his mind went it always returned to the same place.

Eric wasn't that great of a guy. *Hell, he was a dick*, Jay thought. But he was his guide in Brazil, his only link to reality in this foreign land. Without him, he was just another pebble swept away in the sea.

That's when Jay began to hear the voice inside his head.

"Hey, Jay. You didn't even bother saying good morning to me."

Jay turned around in a complete circle, but saw no mouth that spoke the words that he had heard.

"See, you just ignore me. That's typical, Jay."

"I'm not ignoring you. I just can't . . . see you, whoever you are."

"Oh yeah, I forgot I'm dead. Hold on a sec . . . all right, I think we're good."

Jay saw slabs of bloodied meat floating in the air. A few flies hovered around them. He tried rubbing his eyes, but the slabs still floated. It wasn't his imagination, and he hadn't dropped anything even remotely similar to acid since his college days.

"So Eric . . . how do you feel?"

"Dead. That's how I feel. You would think I would have learned my lesson. Watch my temper, all that good shit, but no, here I am. If I could do it all over again I would have probably fucked more whores and then spontaneously combusted."

"Hmmm, well why aren't you in Hell . . . or maybe Heaven? No, no, let's be real, both you and I know you were going straight to Hell."

"Don't be so judgmental, Jay. I know I'm not momma's angel or buttercup, but I did some good things. I did, however, end up in Hell. But the demon was crooked, you know, kind of like cops. Well, we made a deal: a few organs for some time above ground."

"I'm glad I kept some of your organs. Those will come in handy if I ever end up in Hell. And if not, I could always sell them on eBay."

"Good thinking. So where are we off to now?" Eric rubbed what Jay assumed to be an eye.

"To find the hippo and hopefully that will lead us to the researcher."

"Just follow me and everything will be all right."

Jay wanted to believe Eric, but something in the pit of his stomach told him this wasn't going to be the case.

7

Jay and Eric's disembodied organs headed toward the jungle. It was a huge tangle of towering red cedar trees, vines, and a variety of shrubs.

"Hey Eric, did you ever find out what happened to the raggedy man on the other side?"

"Do you really want to know?"

"Yeah. Really."

"Well it turns out the I.R.S. is actually an offshoot of Hell. Over half its profits go to the Devil. Anyway, the Devil got word of the raggedy man skipping out on paying his taxes. Long story short, the raggedy man is now a rag the Devil uses to wipe his balls with."

Jay whistled. "That's harsh. I guess the moral of the story is pay your taxes or else bad things will happen to you."

"Exactly."

Jay used his machete to chop down the man-sized shrubs and ferns that seemed to cover every inch of the ground. His right arm began to tire as the sun slowly sunk on the horizon. He looked over at Eric, who just floated through the plants as if they didn't even exist. He continued hacking plants to clear his path.

"I hate plants," Jay muttered under his breath.

He looked up at the sinking sun. It was blinding as it shone in the sky. He tried wiping the thick coat of sweat off his face, but it only made him sweat more. He dug in his backpack, found a water canteen, and drank the last dregs of water.

A few hours later he passed out.

8

Jay woke chopping at the air. When he realized he wasn't chopping anything he took note of his surroundings.

He was inside a large lime green tent. The walls were thin, almost translucent, but they seemed strong. Shadows passed on the other side of the walls like ghostly apparitions. He wished he still had his machete or at least something with a sharp edge. *What if these people are cannibals?* he thought. *Or worse?*

A shadowy figure came toward the tent. It opened the flap that served as the only entrance and exit. A bronzed elderly man came inside. He was half-naked, wearing only a red and black loincloth. Despite his age, his musculature showed he was still in great shape.

Jay saw the elaborate tribal tattoos covering his wrinkled skin as he came closer. The hippo tattoos especially stood out.

"How are you feeling?" The old man spoke in surprisingly clear English.

"I feel . . . okay for the most part. How did you find me?" Jay felt slightly dizzy.

"One of my wives found you while she was

picking berries earlier this morning." He scratched at his ear.

"What time is it now?"

"Three days have passed." He pulled out an incredibly large black bug and ate it.

Jay's head throbbed at the loss of time.

"Yes. Janossa!" He yelled until a small girl came carrying a glass of water.

Jay thanked the girl before he drank greedily.

"Much better . . . thank you for your kindness. You didn't have to take me in."

"You're welcome. However, the great Lastiz would bring great misfortune down upon our village if we didn't treat you with kindness and respect. You are our honored guest." He smiled.

"The Lastiz? Do you know where they are?"

"Yes. Usually by some water. He roams across the land."

"Is he hard to find?"

"Even I who am of many summers have had a difficult time of finding him, but he can be found using patience and a pure heart. Do you possess these qualities?" His eyes sparked with a pale fire.

"Yes, patience is hard, but I can wait just about forever, and I definitely have heart. So I'm pretty sure I'm pure."

"You have to be completely sure or else there could be grave consequences."

After a few minutes of reflection, Jay replied, "Yes, I am sure."

The old man made his way to exit. "You should get some more rest. You have a long day ahead of you." He exited the tent.

Jay closed his eyes and fell into a deep sleep.

The jungle howled.

9

The next time Jay opened his eyes, he saw a myriad of shadows. They ran back and forth across his vision—blots of pure silence. Without caution, someone jacked up the volume a little too loud. A new song played on his internal radio station—screams accompanied by shadows.

Jay's nose twitched as he smelled smoke and some type of meat cooking. He pulled the flap of the tent back and peaked his head out.

This is what he saw: Natives on fire, running back and forth. Some rolled on the ground, clutching themselves as their skin melted away like wax. Others aimlessly darted back and forth, but they all ended up nowhere, trapped by the jungle's thick vegetation.

Jay spotted an anomaly: two white people amid a crowd of bronzed natives, moving slowly. He recognized them as the old couple from the states. They were toting flamethrowers.

Jay could make out a song underneath the cacophony of screams, a bit of cheerful humming drifting along the wind. It came from the old woman. She had her gray hair drawn back into a tight ponytail, and she wore a frilly polka dot dress that did little to conceal her large figure.

The song gave off the image of her picking weeds out her garden on a nice sunny day. Big weeds which screamed, trying to stay rooted in the earth.

The old man grinned as he pumped out more flames. He had no teeth, just blackened gums.

Jay found the grin sickening. It also fueled the anger inside him. He looked around for any weapons. Then he saw a fat native hugging onto a long spear, looking back and forth in fear and awe.

"Uhhm . . . do you mind if I use your spear?" Jay asked.

The fat native looked shocked. He seemed fragile at that moment, cracked by Jay's words.

"Here. Here. Take it. You can have it. It is all yours now."

"Thanks."

The fat native ran unheedingly into the heart of the flames. Screams followed.

Jay felt the nice, steady weight of the spear in his hands. He looked over at the old man and calculated the distance he would have to throw it. He took a step back and then a step forward, throwing his hip into it and let it loose.

The spear soared through the air, whistling till it hit the old man in the leg. He dropped the flamethrower and clutched his leg. Blood pumped out the wound.

"Shitgodammitmotherfuckergotmeintheleg!" he yelled.

The old woman threw her flamethrower to the side. She waddled over to him and shoved his head into her armpit.

"Robert, are you okay? Did that man hurt you?" She asked while simultaneously stroking his bald head.

"Yeah, I'll survive. We need to regroup."

"Whatever you say, honey." Her voice was soothing.

The old woman picked up the old man, threw him across her shoulder like a ragdoll, and disappeared into the jungle.

The smell of charred flesh had started to get to Jay. He felt his stomach turn sunny side up and he dry heaved. The smoke became heavy, blocking out the sun. His eyes began to smart and he coughed, hacking up a wad of mucus.

Jay covered his mouth and nose with his forearm and began to run. He spotted the old native he met earlier on the ground, clutching his side. He noticed blood, lots of it, and ran over to help.

"Are you okay?" Jay asked.

"No," the old native said before coughing up a bucket of blood. "No, not at all . . . I'm dying."

"Is . . . is there anything I can do for you?" Jay's hands were sweaty.

"It's too late, but I do want you to take this chain off my neck. You are the only one worthy of wearing it."

"Why me?"

"B-Because . . ." the old man said before dying.

Jay looked around to see if anyone noticed the man's passing, but no one seemed to be paying attention because they were too busy dying.

Jay walked up to the old man's limp body and took the golden hippo chain off his neck. He was surprised at its heaviness.

He put it on and felt a chill crawl down his spine.

10

Jay walked slowly, hoping none of the aches he felt were serious. No doctors around for miles and psychotic old people trying to kill everyone in sight. Just great.

Eric materialized in front of a cluster of palm trees. The slabs of meat lazily floated above the ground. This time they were covered with a number of buzzing insects.

"Where the hell have you been?" Jay asked.

"Hold on, what's with all the anger?" Eric replied.

"Well, when you see a tribe get exterminated like pests, you tell me how you're feeling afterward, okay?"

"You could have just called for me. I mean, you are one of my links to this world."

"Links?"

"Yes. You know, things that I'm bound to. Things, people, and places that I'm somehow intrinsically linked to before and after my death." Eric said this as if it was common knowledge.

"What's so important about me? Why am I a link?"

"It's not up to me, never was. I never chose my links. I just live with them. Someone else does all the choosing."

"Well, that's brings us to our second question. Who chooses?"

"Who knows?"

11

Eric and Jay sat under the shade of the canopy overhead. Birds chirped nearby.

"So where to now? I have no idea where we are. Hell, I'm going to get lost just trying to find my way back," Jay said.

"We're going to stay right here and think things through. That would be the best option . . . in my opinion."

"Eric, I value your opinion, but honestly your opinion sucks. We need plans. Concrete plans."

"Well look, my opinion is the only one available. I could leave. Would that make you happy?"

"Yeah. That would make my day. I just need to be alone. Think a little."

"Okay, I understand." While fading away, Eric muttered under his breath, "P-m-s-ing bitch . . ."

Jay sat in silence for a while, his head empty of thoughts. It felt good just to sit and do nothing else.

Then, the image of the old native's face rose out of the green muck of his mind. It was colored with shades of agony and hues of distress. Jay felt his heart sink. At first he tried to ignore the image. He couldn't, however, help but be affected by the man's death. That very moment, he realized the connections between him and death were too familiar to be coincidental. He had a damn good reason to be scared, a reason to pity others. He was only one step away from the edge.

12

Jay walked into a cluster of bushes. He badly needed to take a piss. All day long he had been holding it in. He quickly unzipped his pants and let loose. He savored the sound of his piss hitting the ground.

He zipped up his pants, and out of nowhere, an idea hit him like a coconut falling from above, spilling its juicy contents into the core of his brain.

The chain. The hippo chain was the key to his troubles. All he had to do was figure out what secrets the chain held and he would be on his way to finding the researcher, getting his story, and heading back home.

He, however, knew it was much easier said than done.

Jay sat back down in the shade, chewing on some red berries he had found.

He held the chain in his hand, studying it intently. It glimmered in the light. He traced the curves with his index finger, admiring its beauty and craftsmanship.

The next moment forced him to question his eyes. He rubbed them fiercely, but the sight remained the same. The hippo began to glow, giving off slight warmth and an unearthly radiance. It then began to tug, to pull him to his feet. At first he resisted, not sure what to do. Soon he relaxed and let go. Perhaps it was best to just give in.

Jay was directed where to go, where to turn, and where to jump. He was on autopilot, cruise control. It felt exhilarating; like taking a nice ride, only he didn't have to drive. All he had to do was follow the gentle nudges.

He soon came into a clearing where the cedars thinned. A large lake set in the clearing and inside was a congregation of hippos. They swarmed together in one spot. Or more specifically swarmed around one hippo in particular: the *Lastiz*.

Jay couldn't see it, but he felt its presence. He knew in his heart of hearts, this was what he had been looking for. It felt good to know he had finally reached his destination.

He took a few tentative steps before going into the lake. The water was warm, soaking into his clothes. He didn't mind the wetness; it was strangely calming. He waded farther out into the water, which was now up to his chest. He then stretched his arms out and began to swim. His arms easily cut through the water.

The hippos began to snort and grunt at his approach. They were obviously not too happy to see him and splashed water as he neared. Then, two broke from the group and headed toward him.

He veered off to the right, trying to come up with a plan on the fly. Dread rose inside him.

In his last moment of desperation, he called

for Eric.

Eventually, Eric's disembodied body came into being.

"So, you rang?" Eric asked.

"Yeah . . ." Jay breathed heavily. "I can't believe I'm saying this . . . but I need your help." He felt a dull ache in his muscles.

"Oh, you need my help? What happened to mister I-need-to-be-alone?" Eric teased.

"Eric . . . shut the fuck up and help me."

"Okay, but I won't always be here to do this."

Eric turned hazy once again. Jay briefly felt a wave of terror as he thought Eric was going to fade away. Instead, Eric slipped around and entered Jay's body, filling him with his essence.

Jay felt woozy and almost went under, but Eric kept him above the surface. Eventually, he blurred till he ceased to exist. All he saw was pure white: a beach of everlasting nothingness.

The hippos slowed down, utterly confused by the sudden disappearance of Jay's body. After a while, they returned to the group.

Jay came back, cell by cell till he was complete. He felt out of place. He tested out his hands, tightening them into fists, and opening them to release the tension. After a few seconds, he became accustomed to the idea of *being* again, even though there was something oddly reassuring about floating in a pool of nothingness.

"That was . . . weird," Jay said.

"I'll take your word for it," Eric said.

"What do you mean, you'll take my word?"

"I mean exactly that. There are no hidden metaphors, no deep meaning buried beneath the surface of my words. I just absorbed you into me or vice versa. Either way, I made you disappear. One minute you were here. The next minute you were gone." Eric snapped his fingers.

"So that wasn't the afterlife?"

"No, not my afterlife. And FYI if you haven't figured it out already, the afterlife isn't really my specialty. I'm still learning, picking up bits and pieces as I go along. You know?"

"No, I don't, but I'll take your word for it."

"Hey! Hey now. Don't go using my words. They are copyrighted or are about to be, anyway."

"Yeah. Sure."

Jay continued to swim. Eric continued to hover. They approached the Lastiz with trepidation.

The sheer mass of the hippo was enormous. Jay wished he had his camera with him. He wasn't any good at framing shots, but right about now he had an intense urge to improve.

The Lastiz's golden body rippled in the sun. It gave off an aura of serenity and peace. Jay learned from the past to never trust a gut feeling, especially one strong as this.

The Lastiz's shadow danced upon the small waves of the lake.

Eric spoke up, "Are you ready?"

"I suppose we can't live in between being ready and not being ready forever," Jay said.

"You're right. Let's go."

13

The hippo was silent; it seemed to be posing, showing off its best side for the imaginary cameras flashing shots left and right.

Jay went up to the hippo and caressed its side. It grunted in reply to his touch.

"So, what exactly are we supposed to do, ask where the researcher went?" Jay asked.

"Honestly, Jay, I have no idea. I mean, maybe you should ask it. It could be worth a shot?" Eric laughed.

Jay sighed. "I don't even know why I put up with you, Eric."

"Because I'm all you have in this strange foreign land."

"True. Very true."

"Yeah, I'm like what's his face. I cannot tell a lie."

"I'm sure what's his face never died of spontaneous combustion and came back as a disembodied ghost or whatever the hell you are."

"I can see you're green with envy."

"Either that or it's your bullshit. Take your pick."

"You know what, Jay? That hurt. That hurt me right here." In response, Eric's heart spewed out a geyser of blood.

"Sometimes you need to be hurt to be reminded you're still breathing."

"Oh, look at Jay getting all philosophical on me . . ."

The Lastiz sat down right on top of Eric and Jay, shrouding them in complete darkness. The temperature soared and the smell of shit was horrendous.

"Jay? Jay?!!" Eric called out.

"What? What? I'm right here. I didn't disappear." Jay coughed a few times, straining for air.

"What happened?"

"The Lastiz sat on us. I think we're . . . in its asshole."

"Oh, god, I knew there were things worse than death!"

Jay didn't reply since there was no need. He let the truth settle in before rising to his feet.

"I can't see anything in here."

"Me either." Jay's words echoed through the darkness.

"I would offer my hand to hold, but I don't have any at the moment. Holding my brain would be gay."

"Yeah . . . well . . . hey! Look there's a light ahead. Or something."

There was an abrupt, blinding flash of light.

Eric yelled, taken aback.

Jay didn't say anything. He just blinked his eyes again and again. The moment he opened them, he saw this: a horizon stretching well into the distance. A concrete gray sky with streaks of white running through it. A vast sea of murky brown water and islands separated from one another by the very sea that birthed them.

Jay and Eric sat on one of these very islands. Jay scooped up some of the blood red sand and watched it run through his fingers. "Jesus, this is ..."

"Amazing."

"Took the words right out of my mouth. Who knew another world could exist inside a hippo? Seriously, you know what this means?"

"Yeah, the researcher could be anywhere on this island. Hell, he could be asleep in some bushes and we wouldn't even know."

"You're right. I don't even know where to begin." Jay sat down with a sinking sensation.

"There is that boat up ahead. He could be here." Eric gestured toward the shore.

Jay rushed over to the boat, feeling a bit of giddiness run all over his body. The boat was a dark shade of green and just small enough to fit a single man inside. Waves brushed up against its side, rocking the boat.

Jay stopped. He felt something was off about this. He kneeled down and ran his fingers along the edge of the boat. He moved them downward and felt the rough sides moving slowly in and out. Then, in horror, he realized the damn boat was breathing.

"It's *alive*", Jay muttered.

When he looked even closer, he saw the boat was covered completely in scales. He had thought it was algae, seaweed, or some type of moss.

In the bed of scales, two bulbous eyes blinked and remained open, staring out into the sea. Jay realized it was some type of hybrid—a crocodile/boat, perhaps.

Jay turned toward Eric. "Look at the eyes on that thing."

Eric shrugged what was left of his shoulders. "I've seen bigger."

"Maybe we shouldn't get in. It could be dangerous."

"And this island isn't any less dangerous?"

"It might be a paradise for all we know."

"Or it could be a living hell for all I know, which ain't much. But I have been to Hell and it isn't all sweets and sugar."

"Okay, how about we explore this island a little bit before taking this boat out for a spin?"

"Sounds like a plan, amigo."

Jay walked into the jungle and Eric followed. He worked his way around ancient trees the color of rust, which seemed to stretch into the sky. The same trees had roots the size of giants that dug into the fertile earth.

Jay felt exhausted after what seemed like hours of exploration, so he picked out a clearing and sat on a rock. Eric leaned against a tree, shooing away flies.

"I feel beat." Jay wiped the sweat off his forehead.

Eric picked up a good-sized tree limb off the

ground. Something moved in the canopy, so he poked at the branches he could reach.

"Hey, Jay!" Eric jumped up and down. "I think there's something up here!"

"Well, stop poking it."

A few leaves drifted down. Eric poked it again.

He looked back at Jay, sweat ran down his face. "It's waking up."

Eric screamed and the jungle seemed to do the same.

14

Eric was still screaming his head off.

Jay was doing his best to figure out what exactly Eric was messing with.

A dark object fell from the tree, landing in the thick vegetation. Its body was completely obscured, but Jay could still hear it moving. Then it uttered a deep and throaty growl.

"What the hell did you get us into, Eric?"

"Don't blame me."

"Well, who else should I blame? You're the one who did it."

The thing leaped from its hiding place, revealing an ugly cactus head attached to a grungy monkey's body. Its face formed a shit-eating grin.

Eric threw a handful of rocks at the cactus monkey. Most of them missed, but a few made direct contact. It stumbled backward. Then he threw an even bigger rock, which hit it right in the face. A small cut opened up, tricking blood.

The cactus monkey let out a primordial scream of anger. Jay stepped backward and shoved his hands against his ears.

Eric did the same, but he managed to pick up yet another sharp rock and threw it at the cactus monkey with all his might. It hit the thing right between the eyes. Immediately, it stopped screaming and fell over, the rock lodged in its now bloody face.

"Is it dead?" Jay asked.

"Might be. Let me check." Eric prodded it a few times. "Yep. It's dead."

"Are you sure? What if it comes back like you did?"

"Could happen, but I seriously doubt it."

The trees furiously shook. A few leaves and sharp spines fell down. The jungle filled with the murderous cactus monkey grunts.

"Jay, I think we should leave."

"I'm with you on that one."

Heedless, Jay and Eric ran through the jungle. Eric hopped into the crocodile boat without hesitation. Jay pushed them off the shore and jumped in. They took off toward the horizon with a little help from the wind.

A mass of cactus monkeys popped out from the jungle, running and scrambling full force toward the boat. Jay and Eric paddled furiously to distance themselves from the island.

The cactus monkeys stopped at the edge of the water, as if realizing their efforts were worthless. However, one cactus monkey obviously didn't give a damn about the water or the possibility of drowning. It leaped over the water and landed in the boat.

15

The cactus monkey landed on top of Eric and was scratching his fleshy face apart. Small chunks of skin and cheekbone splattered against a tree.

"Jay get . . . get this . . . thing off me!"

Jay ran over and punched the monkey in the back of the head. He cried out in prickly pain. The cactus monkey glanced back with an air of indifference to the blow and then returned to tearing Eric's face apart.

Jay looked down at his fist, which was now covered in sharp spines, each wound trickled blood.

"Jay!!!"

"Hold on a minute."

Jay looked around for something he could utilize as a weapon. Quickly, he snatched up a paddle and slammed it into the cactus monkey's hairy, spiny back.

It cried out in a scream—grunt and let out a fart before it released Eric's demolished face, now an unidentifiable bloody mess. It fell to the ground like a piece of ham.

Eric picked up his face and put it back on like a lop-sided mask.

The cactus monkey tried to scramble up Jay's leg. Eric came up behind him and grabbed the cactus monkey by the waist and shoulder, and in a blind rage, tore it in half.

A mixture of cactus juice and monkey blood sprayed all over Jay's face till he could barely breathe.

"Jesus Christ, Eric!" Jay spit out phlegm and blood, and wiped some cactus juice out his nostrils.

Eric shrugged his shoulders and grinned. "Shit happens."

16

Jay sat in the boat, delicately pulling spines out of his hands.

"Oh god, this hurts," Jay said.

"Stop your whinin'," Eric said.

"Shit. I'm feelin kinda nauseous." Jay's stomach seemed to do a gold medal worthy somersault, though the little food in his stomach did not have a perfect landing as he threw up brown chunks into the water.

"Felt *cough* like *cough* I threw up my fucking liver. Damn. At least I don't have anything else to throw up." Jay clutched his stomach.

"You've never really been out on water before, have you?"

"Yeah. I like to take a dip in a pool every now and then. And I went fishing once or twice. But, besides that, I don't really see a point in leaving land."

"You really need to get out more, Jay. Live life."

"Yeah . . . maybe."

Jay leaned on the edge of the boat and stared at the shitty brown water, which gleamed like a dirty coin in the sun.

"It's time to go," Eric said.

"What?"

Eric spoke louder. "It's time to go. It's about time we get off this boat. I've been sitting here watching you stare off into space."

"Oh sorry, I didn't know I was daydreaming."

"No problem. I just don't like being here any longer than I have to. This place gives me the creeps."

"You get the creeps? You're dead?"

"Hey, even the dead have things to fear."

17

The island was a picture perfect duplicate of the one Jay and Eric just left. The only difference was this one was accustomed to motion—it moved slowly across the surface of the water like a loose scab.

Jay wasn't sure if he should even set foot on the island. It seemed dangerous. *Someone who threw caution to the wind on a daily basis might go on the island. But not me*, Jay thought. *No siree.*

"Hey Jay, are you coming or what?" Eric said as he floated onto the island. He crossed his arms, or arm, or whatever you would call those loose flaps of skin.

"I'm coming. Just give me a minute. Everyone doesn't float like you."

Eric held a seashell to his ear. Inside, the sea roared and waves crashed upon the shore. Then the sounds began to slowly change into something more alluring. It was as if the waves disappeared and were replaced by moaning. The painful moans of a sweaty woman in labor, ready to give birth. The sweet moans of a young couple making love.

"Hey Jay, you should get a load of these seashells. They're really something."

Jay waved Eric off, thinking seashells were nothing to be excited about.

Eric shrugged. "Your loss".

He picked up another shell, this one being much larger and more elaborately colored. Before he could even put it to his ear, something fell to the sand.

Bending down to pick it up, Eric grabbed the object and saw it was a piece of paper. Probably another lost note from the researcher, Patrick Little.

Jay's interest peaked. "What's that you're reading?"

"Oh, this?" Eric held up the paper. "Nothin'. Just some notes from the researcher."

"Can I have a look at it?"

"Maybe."

"Eric, now is not the time to be playing games."

Eric thought about it and a moment later handed over the page.

"Good move."

"What other moves are there?" He said with a devilish grin.

Jay straightened out the sheet and began to read:

I had no idea.

The implications of this find are, to say the least, enormous. A metaphysician would have a field day with this. Once the outside world gets word, god, it could change everything. But on second thought, I'm not so sure if the world is prepared for this type of change. I'm still getting used to the idea myself.

The concept is what I find most fascinating. An uncharted world within a world. God. I get chills every time I think about it. Hopefully, this one won't go to hell.

The scrawl ended.

Eric spoke up, "So, what do you think?"

"I think he's right. But this doesn't tell us his location. We need something more specific. Something that will lead us straight to him."

"Yeah. What about these footprints?" Eric said smugly.

Jay looked at the impressions in the sand. They formed a trail that led straight into the jungle.

"I really wish I could have my machete right now."

"I really wish I could be alive back in Brazil laid up in bed with a bad Brazilian bitch."

Jay looked over at Eric and shook his head in disdain.

"What? What now? Don't tell me you think any differently. I mean, a machete? Come on now."

Jay began following the footprints. Eric trailed behind, still talking.

18

Eric finally shut up.

Jay, however, began to wish Eric would start again. The absence of sound was getting to him. He kept expecting to hear the wind ruffling through the trees or the caw of a bird—*something*. But all he heard was his footsteps through the brush and the soft murmur of the waves in the distance.

Jay moved his lips together and blew till he found the sound he wanted. He knew whistling would soothe him and keep him rooted in some sense of reality.

He'd been thinking. All his thoughts returned to the same subject, his mind picked and jabbed at it like vultures.

Home, he thought. *How am I going to get back? I never really cared much about life. The newspaper gig was all right. It paid the bills. But there was something missing. Some sort of satisfaction. A sense of ease at the end of the day.*

I need something more.

A sharp sound broke through his thoughts. Not whistling, but something sweeping through the air. The flapping of wings—a great number of them.

Overhead, the canopy slightly swayed in the wind.

"They're coming," Eric whispered.

Jay let out a nervous laugh.

Then *they* came in vast numbers. Millions flew overhead. A black blot imposed on the sky. They resembled birds. The only things missing were skin and feathers. All that remained were charred black bird skeletons, leaving trails of ash behind in their wake.

Their eyes were empty pits of darkness, hollow caves of night. Jay couldn't help but stare. He felt disorientated after a while.

Images began to manifest themselves in the darkness, hazy at first. Eventually, they gained clarity and definition. Jay saw a younger version of himself.

He was lost in the dark. A dark cornfield surrounded on all sides by pale hands. That's what he thought the cornstalks looked like, pale hands reaching into the sky. Stretching, straining, the air was thick with the stench of decay and rot.

Jay continued his way through the field, cringing every time he brushed against a cornstalk. He kept his eyes focused on his house ahead. It continually shifted its shape in the darkness, groaning with its own internal pain. He couldn't tell if what he saw was real or imagined. Both were the same to him now.

The house seemed to sway in the distance. A large chunk of darkness, eating away at the moonlight.

Jay was jerked back from the darkness. Eric was shaking him.

"Jay, Jay? Speak to me!" Eric said desperately. Then, he slapped Jay.

"W—what? Hey, don't slap me." Jay slapped Eric back.

"This is serious, Jay. The birds—or whatever the fuck those things are—are dropping bird shit, and it isn't the kind were used to." He pointed to a plant covered with white crap. At first nothing happened, but the effects became quickly apparent. A fresh wisp of steam rose into the air. The plant began to die, decaying rapidly.

"That's proof enough for me. We need to find some cover."

"I've been telling you this for how long?"

"Just shut up and come on!"

Jay ran with his hands covering the top of his head, knowing it would do absolutely nothing to protect him from the terror above. Still, it was a natural reaction. It made some small part of him, some tiny fraction of his mind, feel safe and secure.

And that tiny comfort was more than enough.

Heavy drops of shit splattered everywhere he turned. They reminded him of missiles, nukes dropping, exploding. Each one had his name written on it and created a fresh grave which called out to him.

Jay ignored the calls. Instead, he focused on the sizzling, snap, crackle, and pop that followed, signaling another small death.

He hurried on with death at his heels and spotted a gaping cave ahead. Eric was almost there, but not quite. Jay caught up in a matter of seconds, driven by the hope of cover. Then he passed Eric, running straight to the finish line. He raised his hands in mock victory as he made it.

He let out a breath of air, put his hands behind his head, and focused on steadying his breath.

Eric came inside a moment later tired as well, and a little red in what was left of his face. He staggered, unsure of his footing, and finally fell exhausted to the ground.

19

"Are you okay?"

"...I don't feel so good," Eric moaned. He tried getting up on his hands and knees, but it was no good.

"Look, let me give you a hand." Jay offered his hand, waiting.

Eric winced as he tried to sit up. He felt something burrowing inside him. It weaved its way effortlessly through his slabs of meat, searching for an exit.

A hoard of flies moved away and dispersed, instinctually aware of what was about to occur.

Eric grabbed Jay's pants leg in a desperate hold. Then he began to groan, trying his damnedest to suppress the excruciating pain. He clutched his chest with his freehand and doubled over. He threw up a watery mix of maggots and long dead butterflies.

"That's nasty." Jay tried to turn his head away, but he couldn't help but watch in sick fascination.

Eric let go of Jay's leg and wrapped both his arms around his stomach. He looked like he was about throw up again. Instead, there was the skull splitting sound of bones snapping, tendons tearing, muscle ripping, and flesh stretching to its furthest limits and finally giving way.

A pale head peaked out, laying its beady black eyes on Jay, which swiveled this way and that. It continued to squeeze its slim, rounded body from Eric's chest till it fell on the ground with a wet smack. It squirmed in its fluids and struggled to move around. Then a pair of thin translucent wings swung out from it back, throbbing with a network of blue veins.

Eric was on his side crying out in post labor pain. His stomach had a hole the size of a fist in it, and it bled non-stop.

The thing managed to hover in the air. The wind blew dust, dirt, and grit all around the cave. Jay marveled in horrific fascination that the thing was actually a giant moth.

He broke out in a cold sweat. He didn't have any weapons to defend himself and Eric was useless, bleeding all over the place.

The moth gained strength and control over its wings and flew out the cave, leaving behind a strong gust of wind and his father cringing in agony.

20

Jay stared at the fire warming his body. Reddish-orange figures shifted and danced inside the flames. It was far from entertaining or amusing, and only emphasized his growing hunger and the agonizing cold.

He looked over at Eric, who slept soundly. He had passed out immediately after giving birth. Jay wrapped his stomach with some large leaves. He didn't want to admit it, but he was glad Eric wasn't dead, again. He had no idea what he would do without some company.

The fire crackled, reminding Jay of candy wrappers. God, he thought with aching pain, *I'd kill for some candy right about now.*

He couldn't remember the last time he had eaten. There was nothing to measure time here. Earlier, he inspected his cell phone and it simply froze, unresponsive to his touch. For some reason, he still kept the thing in his pocket. He could feel its bulk even now.

Outside, the world was dark.

That's how Jay thought of it now. The world. Dark.

He grabbed the note beside him. He traced the torn edges with his finger, enjoying the rough texture. He had stumbled across it while searching for some firewood.

He read it again:

I'm sitting by the shore, cross-legged, writing these notes. Small waves lap at my bare feet. Diamonds of light glitter on top the water. I feel it is important to establish the setting, as it will explain why I write what I write. Moreover, it sets the mood. Now back to the point.

This world is large; perhaps infinite in size. There is no sun, no planets. That is why I ponder the question, where does the day and night come from? Why is there light when there should only be endless darkness?

Through careful study and observation, I have come to the conclusion that this world is lit by the outside. Or, to be more specific, the world outside this one.

You see, there is a day and night here, which can only be explained by the light that comes through the Lastiz's skin. But that brings another question to mind. How does this light get filtered through the skin? There must be muscles and bones to take into account. All of these objects must impede or dim the light in some way.

I will admit that I have no definitive answer to this question-it's pure speculation. On many levels, this world defies all logic. Perhaps it works according to its own mechanics.

Jay stared at the words until they became blurry. He carefully folded the note and put it in his back pocket next to the other sheet. Eric had awoken while he was reading.

"Hey Eric, where do you think he is right now?"

"Who?"

"Who do you think I'm talking about?" Jay asked, slightly angry.

Eric looked innocently at Jay. "The researcher, I suppose."

"You suppose." Jay sighed. "I don't know why I even put up with you, but seriously, answer the question."

"Well, if I was him I'd probably be A: sleeping somewhere safe or B: trying to get some food."

"Hmmm . . . I believe 'A' would be the best answer. I think I need to get some shut eye." Jay sighed. "Tomorrow, we'll search for him and get some food."

He laid down thinking he would have a difficult time resting on the hard, rigid ground. However, he fell fast asleep as soon as he closed his eyes.

21

Jay and Eric walked down to the beach. Eric suggested trying to catch some fish. Jay found a thin branch and tied one of his shoelaces to one end.

"Hey, what's that?" Eric said.

At first Jay didn't know what the hell Eric was talking about, then a moment later he felt stupid as he saw something white among the red sand.

Jay picked it up and dusted the sand off the surface before he began to read.

Due to excessive hunger pains, I had to find a way to catch some food. There seems to be evidence of animal life, feces and such, but no animals have shown themselves. So I went down to the shore and decided to fish. In my youth, I went fishing with my father. However, it has been such a long time since I've used a fishing pole. Now what I had slapped together wasn't exactly the same but close enough.

Instead, I found a long sliver of wood. Regrettably, dire circumstances forced me to pull a lace loose from my shoes. And not just any shoes, my prized 1982 Converses.

I attached the aforementioned shoelace to the sliver of wood with a butterfly knot. I needed some type of bait. Luckily, I came across some small fish. They were scattered throughout the sand. Small in size. Perhaps guppies or some similar variation. They possessed three fins and two beady black eyes.

With some luck and intuition, I attached a fish to the end of my string. I cast my line out and waited. Over time, the heat began to bear down on me. So much so that I had to take off my shirt. I felt embarrassed to show off my flabby chest. But once I realized I was alone, my self-consciousness dissipated.

After a while of baking in the sun, or at least a filtered version of it, I began to doze off. I awoke when I felt a gentle tug at the end of my line. I lifted my head, briefly confused, then I tightened my grip and pulled with all my might. The other end pulled just as mightily.

Finally, I fell on my behind and my shoelace flipped in the air and at the other end a fish was attached. I stared in awe as the fish tumbled ashore. It resembled a salmon; the only difference was this salmon was composed of three "balloons" connected to one another. It was a grotesque sight- the skin stretched over its bulbous frame and the single black eye, which reminded me of soft black stars.

Each "balloon" had gills in the side, which allowed the passage of blue fluids . . . and words.

"If you would be so kind, can you please put me back in the water?" The fish said.

"I'm afraid I can't. I need some dinner," I said.

"Why me? There are plenty of fish in the sea."

"Well, it's survival of the fittest, the circle of life coming full round as they say."

The fish pondered this a bit before speaking. "I suppose you're right. Indeed, I did bite down. And my life would prolong yours as well. I have no regrets. I am yours to do with as you please. Enjoy me."

I was taken aback that this fish would give its own life for another. Not many humans I know would do the same, so I ended its life quickly with the sharp end of a twig. Surprisingly, I found myself wiping a tear away.

I prepared a fire and built a grill of sorts to cook it. The heat felt warm as the day cooled down. I still find it strange and depressing that there is little sunlight.

It didn't take too long to cook. The insides were full of blue meat. I was apprehensive about eating it, but when my belly grumbled I shoved it in my mouth. It tasted like chicken. But not quite the same taste. More like a . . . chicken from the sea. If that makes any sense whatsoever.

After filling myself up, I still had some left over, so I wrapped it up in paper and shoved it into my pocket. I'm sure I will need it later.

When Jay put the paper down, Eric snatched the sheet out of his hand. "Let me see this."

Jay watched Eric's eyes scan the page.

Eric handed the paper back to Jay. "Looks like we'll be having fish tonight."

"Yeah, fish will do." Jay sighed.

"Don't tell me you don't like fish."

"I like fish, just not fishing."

"Why not?"

"I don't have the patience to sit in a boat holding a string in my hand. Waiting and waiting."

"Sometimes the fish is worth the wait."

"Let's just get it over with."

22

Jay tried to take one of Eric's shoelaces, which he didn't need since he floated and never walked, but somehow Eric thought differently.

"I need *that*."

Jay clutched his fist tightly, ready to explode. "How many times do we have to go over this? You don't need this." He dangled the neon green shoelace.

Eric's face creased. "B—but . . . you don't mess with a man's kicks . . . and I just gave birth recently."

"You're fine and this is for both of us. We need some food to survive and this is our only chance. You might even die. Would you like to experience an after death experience?"

Eric's eyebrows lifted in fear. "No, not at all. After death is not for me."

Jay began tying the shoelace to a long branch he found. He felt volcanic anger rise once Eric had begun protesting.

"Hold on. Only on one condition will I grant you exclusive permission to use my shoelace."

"Okay . . . and what is your condition?"

"You must use one of your shoelaces as

well."

Jay looked down at his vintage 1998 black and white pair of Michael Jordans. *This is my life*, he thought. *I need these. Not many exist. And what would MJ think?*

"What would MJ do?" Eric said as if he'd read Jay's mind.

Jay pondered the question long and hard before bowing his head in defeat. He pulled the black shoelace from the hole and had to hold back tears so he wouldn't look gay in front of Eric.

Jay quickly tied the shoelace to Eric's before he changed his mind. And with a flick of the wrist, he cast the line out into the ocean.

"You better have a seat, Eric. It's going to be a long wait."

Eric sat and stared across the surface of the water into the horizon. A few birds soared in the distance, flapping their charred skeleton wings. He shivered.

Jay stared too but directed his on the water. Floating lazily, there were a number of large trees covered in thick layers of green fungus. Others had their roots sticking out of the water like mutilated hands.

Jay hummed a little tune before he felt something pull on his line. He tested it by giving it a hard tug. Whatever it was had some strength because it forced him to stand.

Eric jumped to his feet. "Come on, Jay. You can do this. Just pull."

"Shut . . . up." Jay began to sweat.

Jay pulled harder, putting all he had into it.

His back and shoulders began to throb a few seconds later. Now *I know how Atlas must feel*, he thought as the pain increased tenfold.

With a grunt, Jay leaned backward—digging his heels into the sand. The fish pulled him forward. He fell down face first. Luckily, the sand cushioned his fall.

Inch by inch the fish began to drag Jay into the water. He closed his eyes and unintentionally swallowed some of the bitter tasting sea.

Eric ran over and wrapped his hands around Jay, attempting to pull him back onto the shore. But Jay was much larger than Eric, and the tension on the other side of the line grew taut. Despite the odds, Eric strained and began to take a step back, then another, and then another.

Both Jay and Eric collapsed into the sand, exhausted. The fish popped up in the air. At first it looked like your ordinary trout. Then the fish split itself into four segments for a moment and a second later became whole before landing in the sand. Frenzied, it smacked itself on the sand repeatedly.

"I'm dying," the fish said with a squeaky voice.

Jay said nothing, too tired to speak.

"Why . . . am I dying? What's the purpose of my death?"

The questions were too much. Each one made Jay feel guilty. He wished the fish would just shut up and die.

"Answer me!" the fish demanded.

"Okay, okay. I'm hungry. I don't know

where I can get food. I might die if I don't eat. No, that's a guarantee. I will die, and the same thing might happen to my friend Eric over here." Jay gestured toward a grinning Eric. "The thing is I need to eat you. If there was something else I could eat around here I would, but . . ." he bowed his head in shame.

"Don't worry. I understand your pain. My death will become significant, and I will die happily knowing my life saved the life of another. It will be an honor if you consume me. Just make it quick."

"Okay."

Jay and Eric returned to the cave with the fish in hand. They sat down, and after some rummaging and scuffling, they started another fire.

"Do you know how to cook or even barbecue?" Jay asked.

"No, not without a microwave, toaster, or oven."

"That's not cooking."

"Well, your definition of cooking differs."

"I guess it does."

Jay prepared the fish carefully by shoving a sharp, skinny branch through its soft body. He constructed a little contraption out of branches and seaweed, which hovered above the fire. By the time he had finished and began the nitty gritty part of grilling, Eric had fallen sound asleep.

Jay flipped the fish over back and forth. The simple act of cooking made him feel calm, at ease.

Finally, Jay slapped the fish onto a relatively clean rock with a flat surface. The fish split itself into four equal portions. Happy he didn't have to find something to slice the fish with; he grabbed a piece in his dirty hands and bit down. Sweet juice rolled down his chin, but he didn't care. No one was watching, and the taste was utterly amazing.

Jay stopped himself before he picked up another piece. Eric was sound asleep and he knew it would be wrong to eat everything and not let him have a bite. So he walked over to Eric and nudged his disembodied shoulder.

Eric woke up instantly, drool falling down his lips and never touching his chin because the distance between the two was too great.

". . . Wha . . . do you want?" Eric scratched a slab of meat, which Jay assumed was a thigh.

"The fish is done. Would you like some?"

"Yeah. Is it any good?"

"In all honesty, yes. Very good."

Without further ado, Eric dug in like a hungry pig. Juice and small pieces of fish fat clung to his face, despite his efforts to wipe them away.

"Did you enjoy the fish?"

Eric simply grinned.

23

Jay coughed.

He coughed into his fist till his throat felt dry and gritty. His slick, sweaty hands had trouble holding onto the sheet of paper.

This world is strange. You would have to live here, immerse yourself in this environment to fully comprehend even a fragment of this place.

I have difficulty trying to figure out anything here. Nothing makes sense. The variables are off the charts and there's no way I can begin to make progress without some assistance.

For example, that fish I ate the other day has started to change me. I don't know if my body isn't used to the potency of the food here or what. It's all very troubling. Another possibility is my body decided to reject the food. It recognized the fish as a foreign body, something that would cause harm in the short term rather than the long.

Sadly, the fish has won out, or my body was just too weak. Whatever the case, my body is different. Significantly different. I woke up this morning with a terrible pain in the small of my back. At first, I attributed the pain to sleeping on a hard surface, but I knew that was just me trying to rationalize the unknown.

There are no mirrors and no reflective surfaces, so I used my hands to feel along my back for any bumps. I felt along the bottom of my spine till I came into contact with a small round stub, which I assumed became stuck on my back during my slumber. My mind reeled when I tried pulling the stub and I cried out in pain. The stub was now part of me.

I searched the dusty chambers of my mind for anything that would cause this type of sickness or physical abnormality, but my mind came up short. There was no reasonable explanation, and that was that. But when my hand felt more stubs, bending and unbending on their own volition, I almost had a heart attack.

I realized the stubs were not merely stubs, but fingers. Fingers attached to hands, attached to my back. Somehow, they managed to grow in just a matter of days.

In desperation, I ripped the fingers off my back. I almost blacked out when I was halfway through. I could feel the hot blood running down the base of my spine. And the pain was all there was. It was my lover and my enemy. Pain was my heaven and hell. Pain.

When I finished, I sat on my hands and knees breathing hard and heavy, trying to relax so my heart rate would return to normal.

But the sight, the mere sight of those fingers that grew out my back, made me want to vomit. Still, I managed to hold in my food. The only problem was the longer I stared at the fingers bleeding out onto the beach, the angrier I became. In a blind rage, I scooped up the fingers, disgusted at their touch, and threw them into the sea. Immediately, dark shadows rose up and consumed the fingers. Relief washed over me, relief that I wouldn't have to deal with anything like this ever again.

I knew I was wrong. My denial was the result of a feverish mind. The result of the common man. Humans are forced to rationalize the unknown, the spectacular, anything fantastic just so they can sleep soundly at night. But I knew the scientist in me would win over the fool.

But could the scientist win over the unknown? I still ponder that question. For every discovery made, and though it seems impossible, ten more appear. Maybe I'm just being cynical, maybe not.

I feel I'm cracking up and may never be able to put the pieces together again.

Jay was cold after reading the notes. Frantic, he felt his back as much as he possibly could for any odd stubs or bumps. He couldn't conceive of the horror of having fingers growing out of his back.

Jay knew he ate the fish, every last morsel, and enjoyed it. But now, he began to regret it. *Wait,* he told himself, *there are plenty of fish. What are the chances of me eating the same type Patrick had eaten?*

Still, Jay didn't believe his mind's explanations. He knew it didn't matter what kind of fish he ate. Something was going to happen. Or as the scientist would say: for every action there is an equal and opposite reaction. And it was only a matter of time before the reaction made itself apparent.

24

Jay ripped a thick strand of grass in half and took one half and peeled it in half till it became too small for his fingers to tear. Then he sneezed. Not once or twice, but three times. He felt his nose begin to run.

He wiped his nose with his arm and began to feel sick. Not because of the mucus, but due to the snot-covered crabs on his arm scuttling away.

"What the hell is wrong with you?" Eric asked. "You have crabs coming out of your nose."

Angry, Jay was about to say something smart, but fear overcame the anger when a few more crabs fell out of his nose.

"Here's a tissue. Blow your fucking nose," Eric said.

Jay snatched it and blew. He sounded like an elephant. He opened up the tissue and saw four crushed crabs stuck in mucus, bleeding out the last dregs of their lives.

The tickling ceased in Jay's nose though. To be safe, he blew two more times. When nothing came out, he released a sigh of relief.

"Are you all right?" Eric asked.

"No. It's that fish we ate. Apparently, it changes us," Jay said.

"No, that was just a fluke."

"It wasn't a fluke. Those crabs are a direct result of eating that fish. Kind of like a nasty side effect. It even happened to the scientist. Check it out." Jay handed Eric the notes.

Eric's eyes skimmed over the paper. "It looks like you're right. But I don't know if the fish can affect the dead."

"For your sake and sanity, I hope it doesn't."

25

"How are you feeling? Any different?" Jay asked.

"Uhmm . . . as far as I can tell, no. Everything feels the same. I wish I was alive though," Eric said.

"Why? Life isn't all that."

"Well, for instance, taking a piss isn't that fun when your penis is slowly decaying. Piss gets all over the place."

Jay looked disgusted. "I guess I shouldn't have asked."

"No, you should watch what you say and what comes out your nose."

Jay began picking his nose, checking for any stray crabs.

"Calm down, Jay." Eric patted him on the back. "I was just pulling your leg."

Jay pushed him away. "This isn't a fucking game. We've been here for days and we still haven't found the researcher. To top it all off, I have crabs coming out every orifice of my body."

"Sounds like somebody could use a drink."

"Yeah. A beer sounds good right about now."

"Look, Patrick Little has to be close. He's

only human. He has to rest. He has to eat. We'll catch up to him."

"I hope so. I'm tired of this wild goose chase."

"Yeah, but goose aren't so bad. The geese are the ones you really have to look out for."

Jay didn't say anything. That was the best thing to do, he figured. If he responded, the day would only end in a headache. And he really didn't need another headache.

Leaves crunched followed by a loud snap of a branch. Someone was coming. Jay put his index finger up to his lips. Eric nodded. They snuck behind a large rock that resembled Sylvester Stallone's nose.

After a few moments, which felt like a few eternities, a large bush parted, and a man in tattered clothing stumbled out into the clearing. His clothes which used to be an idealistic white were now smeared with blood, dirt, and god knows what else. Even behind his coke bottle glasses, anyone could see his eyes were bloodshot. And those eyes kept looking, surveying his surroundings.

He spoke softly. "It's safe. You can come out now."

Jay's eyes bugged out and Eric began to freak. Jay wasn't sure if Patrick spotted them. He was sure they were well hidden from view, but . . . you could never tell. Maybe Patrick could hear them.

Jay felt something shatter inside the moment the woman came out from her hiding place. Her skin was alabaster white and her eyes were a swirling mass of colors. A man could drown in those eyes . . . willingly. Though the thought chilled him to the core, he continued to gaze at her in awe.

She wore a green cloak over her lithe frame. It ruffled in the wind, revealing the bare skin of her thighs. Jay tried to check himself before he began to fall too far. He knew there was a big difference between love and lust.

He looked over at Eric, who was mesmerized by the unknown beauty. He waved his hand in front of his glazed eyes.

Nothing.

Jay whispered, "Eric, Eric. Snap out of it."

Eric looked over, and drunkenly said, "I think I'm in love."

26

"So what's the plan?" Eric asked.

"We should follow and take it from there," Jay said.

"Why do I have a bad feeling about this?"

"Well, do you have any better suggestions?"

Eric put his finger on his chin to emulate deep thought, but his finger kept falling off his hand. "No."

"That's what I thought."

27

Jay and Eric followed about ten paces behind Patrick Little and his unknown companion.

Eric whispered, "I'm not sure if this is such a good idea. I know we have to find him and bring him back, but can't we just say we couldn't find him?"

Jay considered it. He thought about the constant scampering of the crabs and how hungry he felt, but his need to see things through to the end overrode Eric's suggestion. "No. We need to get Patrick and leave. You can't wait a little bit longer?"

"I guess," Eric said, somberly.

Jay shoved Eric onto his back and covered his mouth.

"Sssshhhh."

Eric nodded.

Patrick paused and looked around as if he had heard something and then continued along the beaten path. Eventually the path curved and seemed to end in thick undergrowth. However, he pushed it aside easily, gesturing for the woman to go through. She smiled and went inside. He followed, and the undergrowth sprung back to its original position.

Eric began to hurry toward the entrance. Jay

grabbed a thick slab of meat and threw it to the ground. The rest fell on top with a groan.

"Stop, we can't go in there all willy nilly. Maybe we should wait until one of them comes out."

"Jay, we can't wait. We have him right in our grasp. All we have to do is go in there and introduce ourselves. Everything will go smooth as a whistle, just watch and learn."

"Okay, okay. The only thing I ask is that you do all the speaking."

"It would be my pleasure."

Jay headed toward the entrance with Eric in tow. He was about to move the branch aside, but felt a hot breath on his neck. Angry, he turned around, ready to give Eric a piece of his mind.

A fist smashed his face in. Everything became blurry as he fell to the ground.

28

Jay woke with a start. A firm hand pushed him back down. He was in a dimly lit enclosed space. Giant mushrooms vaulted into the sky on all sides, blocking out the light. However, thin shafts of illumination broke through the darkness here and there.

"Keep your mouth shut and don't move," a stiff voice warned.

Jay nodded. He was aware of the figure's movement but couldn't make out any distinct characteristics. A moment later, the man stepped into the light. He wore a pristine black suit, but he also wore a cape over his head, which draped down his back. No, it wasn't a cape . . . it was skin—the raggedy man's raggedy skin.

Jay's skin crawled at the grotesque sight.

What the hell? This must be an I.R.S. agent, Jay thought. *What do they want with me?* I paid my taxes.

Mr. Pristine walked over to a large pile of bones Jay had failed to notice until now. He picked up a large concave bone, but something wasn't to his liking, so he tossed it back on top the pile. He snatched a smaller one and licked his lips before biting off a chunk of the bone and spitting it to the ground. He sucked the marrow out in a matter of seconds.

"Ahhhh . . . that is fine cuisine, if I must say so myself."

Mr. Pristine winked at Jay and disappeared back into the darkness.

Jay heard muffled voices, obviously discussing him. He watched the man come back with another guy who wore a black suit, but his was too tight, slightly ruffled, and not so pristine as his companion's.

"I see you're awake, Mr. Robbins. This pleases me immensely." Mr. Tight spoke in a clear, concise tone.

He also wore a blotchy discolored skin over his back. This one belonged to Eric.

"Where the hell is Eric and why are you wearing his skin?" Jay demanded.

Mr. Tight backhanded Jay, obviously displeased. He frowned. "Mr. Robbins, I do believe you were instructed not to speak, and what did you do? You spoke. And therefore you had to face the consequences of my hand smacking you. Now, don't speak again unless spoken to."

Jay spit out some blood and nodded.

Mr. Tight pulled out a cigarette and lit it.

Mr. Pristine glared at him. "Why must you smoke those cancer sticks?"

"When I get stressed, I smoke. And this chap is stressing me immensely."

"You heard him. Why are you stressing people out?"

Jay tried opening his mouth to respond.

"Stop. Hold that thought. He is an innocent man. I mean, yes, he has murdered a few people here and there, but you don't skip on your taxes. That is just plain wrong and this isn't a question of ethics, either."

"I didn't skip out on my taxes."

"Yes, yes that is what they all say. The same tired drivel. In all honesty, I don't give a diving damn if you paid or not. You saw us kill the raggedy man and that is reason enough."

Jay sighed, finding this whole predicament puzzling.

"Look, I'm going to go speak to your friend because you're boring me. My partner will watch you in my brief absence."

Mr. Tight smiled with pleasure. Jay noticed with disgust that the guy had crooked yellow teeth. He would've thought these two had perfect smiles, considering the government paid for them.

Mr. Tight stared at Jay as if he were an interesting animal at the zoo, a freshly opened exhibit the public couldn't wait to see, but upon seeing it, was disappointed.

Jay felt weird watching this guy stare at him. He wished he could poke the fucker's eyes out.

Mr. Tight crushed his cigarette with his heel and strode over to Jay. He snatched the notes sticking out the back of Jay's jeans.

"What do we have here, huh? Love letters perhaps? Or maybe something juicy like a diary?"

Jay's heart leaped. "No, give those back! I need them!" He stood to face his interrogator.

Casually, Mr. Tight pulled out an AK-47. He looked amused, regarding the dread in Jay's face. "Oh, these must be important. I was just going to toy with you, but you have my curiosity piqued."

He read over the notes in a matter of minutes. Then he looked up. "Hhmmmm . . . these are quite interesting, but ultimately have little significance to me."

He whipped out his lighter with his free hand and put the flame under the notes.

"No! Don't do it! Please!"

Mr. Tight simply laughed.

A high-pitched scream rose in the darkness.

Both Mr. Tight and Jay looked up in fear.

29

Mr. Pristine and Eric ran through shafts of light and were swallowed by darkness the very next instant. They both wore masks, one full of fear and the other full of frustration.

Mr. Pristine looked back in absolute horror, watching the seething mass in the darkness, shooting wildly. He had cuts all over his face. His suit hung in tatters and no longer quite so pristine.

"Run, Jay! Run for your life!" Eric yelled floating quickly as he possibly could.

Cactus monkeys rained from above. Mr. Pristine managed to take out a few before one cactus monkey ruthlessly tore his arm from his body. Blood gushed from his shoulder socket, spraying the base of a mushroom a vivid red.

Jay took off running. Every minute was essential, every second precious. The cactus monkeys were only going to spend so much time on Mr. Pristine and Mr. Tight, and then begin the search for him.

He glanced back and saw Mr. Tight shooting into the heart of the cactus monkeys and using Mr. Pristine's limp body as a shield.

He continued running blindly, ferns and branches scratched his face, tearing holes through his shirt. Thick vines hung like snakes. He wondered if this darkness would ever end.

Jay was ready to give up when he spotted a small pocket of light in the distance. He picked up his speed, hoping this meant escape. He broke through the cramped space into a small clearing. Light poured down on him.

He dropped to his knees and kissed the ground again and again.

"Jay, when you and the ground are done smooching you can come hide over here," Eric said.

Jay blushed in embarrassment and entered the bush. He listened to his own heavy breathing and the gunshots ringing in the distance. Over time, the shooting stopped, and all that remained was an eerie silence.

30

After what felt like forever, Jay assumed it was safe enough to poke his head out from the bush. He looked from side to side for any movement.

Nothing stirred.

"Eric, I think it's safe."

"What if it's a trap?"

"I doubt they're that smart."

"Okay, but let's hurry. I don't like being around here."

They worked their way through the jungle and the humidity. Jay smiled once he recognized his surroundings.

"Eric, I think we're okay. Remember Patrick and that girl? I think their hideaway is somewhere around here."

"Yeah, this does look familiar."

Jay worked his way up a sloping hill. "So, what happened back there? The last thing I remember was looking back and *boom*. Nothing."

"Well, they snuck behind us. One of those guys clasped his hand over my mouth and shoved a gun against my temple. I'm surprised they could find it. Anyway, the other guy threw a nasty right hook to the back of your head. You slumped over and fell to the ground. Then they dragged you into their little hideout. Not too soon after that, you came to."

"Damn. We need to be more careful, watch our backs. But at least they're dead."

"Yeah, good riddance."

"Hey, it's right over there!" Jay pointed a few feet ahead.

Eric ran over and Jay followed, going in headfirst. The first thing he saw was a fire, a great fire that lit the cave. It threw shadows upon the large walls, dancing this way and that. Two silhouettes sat side by side on a pair of large rocks.

Eric walked a few paces ahead and made the fatal mistake of clearing his throat. "Uhmm . . . hi, my name is—"

Patrick jumped up and whipped out a pistol from his back pocket, pointing it directly at Eric's head.

"Put your hands up . . . or whatever the fuck you call those things!" Patrick said.

Eric obeyed without hesitation. "Hey, there's no need to be hostile!"

Patrick looked Eric up and down; his face became a mixture of disgust and pity. "Shut up! Just shut up! I'm calling the shots here."

Jay came out of the shadows with his hands up.

Patrick jumped back and swung his gun in the direction of Jay's face. "Who's this? Who the fuck is this? Somebody better answer me. Now!"

Jay put his hands out and spoke in his most calm voice. "My name is, Jay Robbins. I'm a journalist. I work for the *Superfly Times*. Eric and I were sent here to find you."

"Well, it looks like you found a whole lot more than you bargained for." Patrick wiped away the sweat from his forehead.

The woman curiously watched the whole affair unfold without saying a word. When she did begin to speak, everyone grew quiet and focused on her.

"Stop. All of you. Patrick, put the gun away. You two need to come here and have a seat by the fire."

Patrick acted shocked, and his face showed his feelings were slightly hurt. "But—"

"There's nothing to be afraid of. Well, at least not in the cave and not at the moment. Everyone have a seat. I'm beginning to get impatient."

The sweetness of her voice carried the slight potential for a venomous bite if crossed. Jay and Eric cautiously approached the fire and sat opposite the woman.

Patrick put his pistol away and sat down beside the woman.

"I trust you two. Want to know why?" she asked.

Eric stayed silent.

After a moment Jay spoke up. "Yes."

"That chain around your neck. I gave it to a man who accidentally stumbled into this world. He had a pure heart. He saved me once, long ago, and that is why I gave it to him as a gift. It protects whoever may wear it," she paused, and stared into the distance. "I do have a question, how did you come to acquire this chain?"

Jay felt the chain around his neck. Somehow, he managed to forget its presence. He had worn it so long it became another part of him.

"The man saved me. I almost died, but he nursed me back to health. An old couple that had been trying to kill me on my journey here exterminated the whole tribe. It was too late for me to do anything, but I did find the old man. He gave me this chain. And now I know why."

The woman seemed to reflect on this before she spoke once again. "That is a tragic end. He will be remembered. I will see to it. Anyhow, introductions are in order. My name is Promethia. And you two are?"

"My name is, Jay."

Eric had trouble speaking, but on his fourth try the words finally came out nice and easy. "And mine is, Eric."

"Simple names, but fine nonetheless. What is your purpose in being here?"

"Basically, our purpose is to find out what happened to Patrick Little."

Patrick was busy cleaning his glasses. "Well, it looks like you succeeded. But how do you plan on getting us out of here unscathed?"

"I haven't really thought about that, but I do have a question," Jay said.

Promethia urged him on. "Go ahead."

"What is this place? I mean we're stuck inside of a hippo and—"

"This place, this *world* is called Apeiron. It has existed for an incredibly long time and it will continue existing till the end of time. Sometimes people stumble across this world in the most unexpected of places. You just happened to do it by means of a hippopotamus."

Patrick took off into the darkness to scribble more thoughts on his pad.

Jay still felt a little confused, but got the gist of it.

"Don't worry about it. It's of no significance to you. Excuse me, but I do need to get some rest. You two are welcome to stay the night."

"Thanks," Jay said.

"Much appreciated," Eric said.

Jay and Eric settled themselves in the best they could, and in no time they were knocked out cold.

31

Something cracked loudly.

Jay rolled over and tried to go back to sleep, but when he heard that crack again he sat up. It sounded like a giant watermelon had been dropped from a twenty story building in a world full of silence.

Eric was sound asleep, dreaming of sexy dead prostitutes, Jay imagined.

"Eric, wake up."

Eric moaned and stretched.

"I mean it!"

Eric opened part of one eye and smiled.

"Okay, okay. People can't get a good rest these days." Eric wiped the sleep out of his eyes.

Crack.

Eric flinched. "W—what the hell was that?"

"I don't know, but we're about to find out." Jay stretched his weary limbs.

Jay ran outside the cave. Rain pounded the ground. He licked his lips and was surprised to find a faint taste of pineapple.

Crack.

For a brief moment the world lit up as if someone pulled switched on a light and then turned it off the very next instant.

Lightning. Thunder.

Jay ran back inside, his clothes soaked in under a minute.

"So what's going on?" Eric asked.

"It's raining bullets out there." Jay shivered before continuing. "Looks like we have a thunderstorm on our hands."

"And no umbrellas."

"Hey, where's Patrick and Promethia?"

Eric shrugged. "I have no idea. They should be somewhere around here, though."

"I'm going to kill somebody if they've moved on someplace else. I mean, we just had him last night. Right there in our hands and he slipped away.

Jay slowly approached. Patrick had his back turned, obviously wanting some alone time.

"Hey . . ." Jay stopped in his tracks as he got closer to Patrick.

Patrick didn't have a shirt on. A pair of hands rooted in his back had been digging into his shoulder blades, desperately trying to claw their way out. Dirt, blood, and grime caked the nails. Other hands were content with just flexing a finger while some chose to stretch, trying to escape the prison of flesh to which they were caged.

Patrick turned his head over his shoulder and looked at Jay with indifference before speaking.

"I guess they're not too pleasing to the eye, eh?"

"I-I . . . didn't mean to. I mean . . ." Jay said,

not knowing what to say. He felt the same way when he looked at a burn victim or the morbidly obese, sickened and horrified—uncomfortable at the sight. No matter how hard he tried his eyes returned to the same place, staring.

"Don't be ashamed. I have no qualms about who I am or what I've become. I'm learning to deal with it, if there is a way to deal with it."

Jay swallowed hard. "I have a problem too."

"What's your problem?"

"Nothing huge. Just crabs."

For a moment Patrick didn't react. His body stood amazingly still. When he finally moved, Jay couldn't believe it.

Patrick's head swayed from side to side, then forward and back like a Bobblehead. Jay was sickened for a brief moment as he was reminded of the dead cab driver. Then Patrick's thin mouth opened wide, and a shrill laugh rolled out.

Jay began to laugh as well when his own words finally dawned on him.

"Crabs," Patrick said wiping away his tears. "Oh, that was great."

Jay sneezed. Two mucus covered small crabs fell to the ground and scuttled away in search of darkness.

Immediately, Patrick's laughs were silenced by the mere sight of the crabs. "You weren't lying, were you?"

Jay shook his head. "No, not at all."

"Well, it looks like this island affects everyone, or at least us outsiders," Patrick said. He grabbed a small notepad out of his back pocket and scribbled some quick thoughts.

Promethia walked over.

"Why, good morning. How are you two doing?"

"Morning. I'm okay," Patrick said.

"Good morning. I'm all right, but I was wondering what exactly is up with this storm?"

"Storm?" Promethia's brow creased.

"Yes, there's thunder and lightning. Rain's coming down hard," Jay said.

"No . . . it doesn't rain or storm here. Something's terribly wrong," Promethia said.

"What should we do?" Patrick asked.

Promethia's usually strong voice shook a little. "There's nothing we can do. I think it's because of *him*."

"Because of me?" Jay asked.

"No, neither of you. It's because of Z. That's all I can tell you. But if that is the case, then we need to prepare ourselves."

"You should probably wake your friend." Patrick scrubbed at his glasses nervously.

"I'll do that. Thanks," Jay said.

Jay's thoughts were shaken. He didn't know what to think because this had never happened to him before. He relied on past experience to dictate his next moves. Now, there was nothing to fall back on. Every decision seemed flawed and bound for failure. He was content to focus on one thing and that was waking up Eric.

Jay grabbed hold of Eric's shoulder and shook it gently.

Eric moaned.

Jay shook him even harder.

Eric's eyes snapped open. "Not again."

"Why'd you go back to sleep?"

"Because I saw the opportunity and seized the day."

"Next time you'll be seizing my fist. Get up, something's wrong with this weather."

"What?"

"The rain, the thunder. It never happens here."

"Fuck."

32

"Everyone should leave," Promethia said.

"What about you?" Patrick asked.

"I don't matter. I'm bound here."

"I think someone should at least stay behind and watch over you. I mean . . . what about the *eggs*?" Patrick asked.

"Grab them and leave," Promethia said, angrily.

"What eggs?" Jay asked.

"Fuck. They weren't supposed to know," Patrick said.

"Well it's too late now. They're actually better off knowing. They can help us," Promethia said.

"Okay. You're right."

Jay stood there waiting for an explanation.

Patrick stepped forward. "I'll make this quick. There are a number of fundamentally important eggs we've been hiding in this cave. They hold newborn worlds inside their shells and we have to protect them at all costs."

"Uhhmm . . . okay. I'll help," Jay said.

Patrick disappeared into the shadows.

"Good, you and Eric can be very beneficial to us. It is of great importance these eggs be taken care of or else your world and many others could fall into chaos," Promethia said.

"No problem, but how exactly would these eggs do what you say?" Jay said.

"It's very complicated. Everything is balanced. If one of these eggs is destroyed, your world will be affected in a negative fashion as well."

"Okay, that makes sense. I'll try my best to help."

Jay and Eric went into the shadows, navigating the rocky terrain.

"Hey Pat, where are you? We came to help," Eric said. His voice echoed off the walls of the cave.

Jay hit him in the shoulder. "Cut that out."

"Sorry," Eric whispered.

There was no reply. But Eric and Jay caught a glimpse of his thin, hunched-over frame.

"Hey Patrick, Promethia sent us to help," Jay said.

Patrick wiped his eyes and wiped them again. When he was done he turned around. His eyes were red and bleary. "Hey . . . I got something in my eye. Yeah . . . the eggs. Just stuff them in your pockets. They're very tough, so don't worry about dropping them."

The eggs were stacked in one large heap. Each one resembled a yellowed, oversized chicken egg. Jay, Eric, and Patrick stuffed a number of eggs into their pockets. An uncomfortable silence fell about the room.

Finally, with what seemed like a series of bite-sized decades, all three left with heads hung low. A sense of melancholy washed over Jay and he saw it affected Patrick and Eric the same way.

Promethia stood at the entrance, waiting patiently.

"So, this is goodbye then?" Jay said.

"Yes. Goodbye, it was a pleasure meeting you two." Promethia hugged Jay tightly. He smelled a strange, alluring fragrance. It made him feel slightly dizzy. Then she hugged Eric.

Patrick's eyes met Promethia's for a brief moment.

"I . . . think I'm staying behind."

Jay expected Promethia to lash out when he saw the fire rise in her eyes. Then it died down into embers of green light.

The rain came down in big fat drops in the background.

"Okay, you can stay, but the rest of you must leave quickly. The world is falling apart," Promethia said.

"Okay, we're leaving. Goodbye."

Jay and Eric left, going out into the heavy rain. As they distanced themselves from the cave, Jay looked over his shoulder once. His eyes fixed upon one large silhouette, obviously the shapes of Promethia and Patrick combined into one.

"How are we going to find our way out in this mess?" Eric said, trying to keep the rain out of his eyes.

"We'll find a way. I'm sure of it. Either that or get killed in the process."

33

Thunder rocked the world, sending vibrations under Jay's feet. He slipped, but leaned into Eric for much needed support.

"Fuck. When is this ever going to stop?" Eric shouted, trying to be heard over the rain.

"It won't! Just deal with it!" Jay shouted in reply.

A hand clasped around Jay's mouth and shoved him into a puddle. He turned around and saw Mr. Tight grinning wildly.

Crack.

It was dark, but during that moment of lightning and thunder, Jay couldn't miss the mass of cactus monkey skins on Mr. Tight's back teetering dangerously from side to side. It must have towered eight feet high. He was hunched over from the heavy load on his back.

"I-I thought you were dead," Jay backpedaled.

Mr. Tight took a step forward. "You thought wrong. I showed those fuckers who was boss. Now I'm going to kill you and eat every sweet bone in your body!"

A large shadow descended on top of Mr.

Tight. Jay's eyes adjusted to the darkness and through the heavy rain he saw a giant moth wrapping its massive wings around Mr. Tight. The moth slowly rose into the sky. Mr. Tight screamed and yelled to no avail. Eventually, the darkness swallowed them both.

Something fell on the ground with a heavy thump.

Jay took a cautious step forward and glanced at the object. It was Mr. Tight's head, but no body. His face was frozen in fear and terror.

Something else fell from the sky, landing with a splash.

"What the hell?" Jay looked down.

Mr. Tight's bloody torso.

Eric yelled out as a thigh and chunks of flesh fell on top him. He slipped and fell into a puddle.

"Jesus Christ!" Eric threw the thigh off his face.

Jay jumped out the way as a tree almost crushed him under its immense weight. He watched in awe while trying to regain his footing as other trees fell in a domino effect.

More stuff fell from the sky, smashing into oblivion upon impact. Fruits, plants, and cactus monkeys.

Some of the objects from the sky steamed as they soared downward.

Eric sniffed the air. "Is that? Yes, I think it is. Meat."

"You're right. It is meat."

Jay stared at one slab of meat, which

steamed and bubbled. Grease ran down the length of its body.

"Slabs of meat. Falling from the goddamn sky. This must be what butchers dream of at night," Jay muttered.

"Come on. This place is falling apart!" Eric yelled.

Once again, Jay looked upward, shielding his eyes with his hand. The only difference from before was the gaping holes in the dark sky. He felt an inexplicable dread rise from his gut. Eventually, it forced its way through his pores and covered his body in a cold sweat.

"Jay?" Eric said showing fear in his eyes. "Are you okay? You're trembling."

"I . . . don't know."

Jay fell to the ground, all the time aware of a terrible, wracking pain. He had no chance, no say in the matter because it was over before it had barely began.

34

Jay woke, vaguely aware of a dull throbbing inside his head. But he also felt pain surge throughout his legs, his neck, his shoulders, and his back. Especially, his back.

"Ughh . . . Jesus Christ," Jay muttered.

He put a hand to his head and rubbed it across his face. Quickly, he snatched his hand away and stared intently at his palms, expecting to see smears of his face.

Jay took a deep breath of relief and inspected himself. He was covered in red. Completely and utterly covered in blood among other bodily fluids.

He tried to move, but realized he was stuck in a massive pile of hippo guts.

He began to panic, feeling slightly claustrophobic, but managed to calm himself down.

Then he noticed Eric nibbling on a thick piece of hippo meat, and he seemed to be enjoying its unique flavor.

Eric caught Jay's eyes fixed on his back. He quickly spit out the meat. "Ackk . . . nasty shit. Have no idea how that got in my mouth."

"I saw that."

"Saw what?"

"Saw you eating hippo guts."

Eric looked saddened by these words. "Oh. Well . . . I was hungry."

"Okay."

"Let's get out of this shit and leave. I need . . . I don't know what I need. I just need something. Maybe a drink. Let's go."

After a few minutes of struggling to get each other out of the guts, they finally succeeded. Eric picked a piece of hippo meat out of his hair and slipped it in his mouth when Jay wasn't looking.

Jay snickered . . . till he noticed the beach chairs sitting along the riverbank. And after staring even more closely, he noticed two figures sitting on the chairs. Two figures who moved in the slowest manner possible. He realized they were the murderous old couple.

He felt the need to run over and smash both in the face.

But he held himself back when he saw each cradled an elephant gun on their laps. The old lady stared at hers, massaging and caressing it as if it were her own child. The old man looked blank and detached.

"Hold on, is that who I think it is?" Eric asked.

"Yes. It is."

"So what's the plan? Run in the opposite direction?"

"No, we don't run. Just like my uncle Jack told me, 'Son, sometimes a man has to stand tall even in short times.'"

"Uhmm . . . okay."

"Listen. We're going to go over there. Peacefully. And just talk it over with the two of them." Jay struggled to believe his own words.

"Hopefully, they don't talk with their guns first instead of their mouths."

35

Jay headed toward the old couple with more than mere gusto. He had a pep in his step and a sour taste in his mouth. Eric simply followed in silence.

The old couple took note of the dirty man and his ghostly friend who was dirty too, but not quite as dirty as his companion. The woman turned toward her husband and licked her dry, chapped lips, and said, "It's time to clean house."

She cocked her gun. And the old man did the same.

Jay and Eric stopped in their tracks immediately, paralyzed by the mechanical cycling of the guns being locked and loaded.

"We're fucked. We're fucked—we're fucked—we're fucked," Eric said over and over.

"Shut up."

The old woman lifted herself from the chair with the utmost slowness. There was a deafening crack. Each movement took forever to complete. It was as if her joints didn't know how to loosen themselves from their present state of stiffness.

She took her time, which she was running out of, making her way toward the two men. She spit on the ground before shoving the butt of her gun into one of Eric's slabs of meat—his face.

"Ghost. Undead heathen. You're nothing but cum on the devil's balls. I've killed many of your kind before, and I'm prepared to perform an encore," she growled.

Eric shivered.

Jay was glad he didn't have the gun in his face. He probably would have pissed himself.

"Now listen here and listen good. The two of you are coming with me and my hubby over there. And if you give us any shit, then you'll end like that elephant over there. Comprehende?"

Both Jay and Eric were too shocked to protest.

She gun butted Eric. "I said do you understand?"

"Yes. Yes, ma'am," Eric said.

"Yes," Jay said.

The old woman walked up to Jay with a grin on her face. He noticed she was missing teeth. The few teeth she had left were crooked and yellow. She slowly raised her left hand as if she were about to point at something in the distance. Instead of pointing, she grabbed the elephant gun and swung it into the back of Jay's head. It was all over before he could react.

36

Jay woke, but he kept his eyes closed. He wished he could just keep them shut. The darkness beneath his eyelids was much better than whatever waited for him outside.

He opened his eyes after much debate and boredom. The first thing he saw was the steel bars. The second thing he noticed was the fact he was trapped inside these said bars. Finally, he noticed another cage besides his own and the figure inside to be none other than Eric.

"Eric!!" Jay shouted clutching the bars of his cage.

"What?" Eric shouted back.

"Where the hell are we?"

"Guess."

Jay felt that all too familiar rage start to boil over, but managed to keep it in check and began to think instead. He felt a little dizzy and his ears were all out of tune. There only was one place this strange occurrence happened: the air.

An airplane. The old couple had put Eric and him inside an airplane or maybe even a private jet. Before this whole ordeal, Jay never had any problems with old people. *Now I can't keep them from shoving a gun down my throat.*

"So, did you figure it out?" Eric asked.

"Yes and no," Jay said.

"You must be a little slow."

"You're lucky I'm inside a cage. Or else I'd slowly rip your body limb from limb."

"I was only joking. Anyway, what's on your mind?"

"Well, I know we're in an airplane or jet of some kind. This must be the cargo hold. The thing that has been troubling me is, why? Why are we in this situation in the first place? This was only supposed to be a news story. But now, now it's gotten out of control. It's so much more than a news story. I just can't seem to fit it all together."

"Same here."

Jay doubted Eric was thinking the same thing, but he shrugged it off.

There was some turbulence and the airplane rocked from side to side. Jay held on to the bars for stability.

"Fuck!" Eric yelled.

"You all right?" Jay asked.

"Yeah, I think so. Just bumped my head."

"You probably deserved it."

"What's that you said?"

"Nothing. Nothing. Just the wind."

"Oh, okay."

After some time of silence, Jay heard Eric vomiting. And not too soon, he caught a whiff of whatever Eric had just thrown up. It smelled sort of like seafood and shit.

"Oh, god . . . goddamn hippo guts. Knew I

shouldn't have eaten any." Eric moaned.

Jay felt lightheaded. At first, he thought he was going to be okay until that familiar dizziness started to absorb him. He closed his eyes and blacked out.

37

Jay woke for what felt like the millionth time, but he knew time had passed—a whole lot of time. He felt the gritty beard that had begun to grow as he ran his hand across his face. And he was too aware of the grime that had been building up on his teeth. He didn't even want to know how bad he smelled. A shower felt unattainable, just another pipe dream.

"Is he awake?" An old voice said.

Another voice joined in, sounding female, "Yes. Yes he's moving around. We should stick a pin in him."

A smooth voice began to speak both familiar yet oddly distant. "Not yet, Mrs. Hayes. All in due time. I have to finish wrapping some things up first, and then you two can have all the fun you want."

"Wha—What's going on?" Jay said.

"Put him in the chair." The smooth voice demanded.

The old man and woman had an amazing amount of strength for their respective ages. Jay thought his weight would break their arms like twigs, but he was wrong. Like a little kid, they grabbed hold of his arms and pulled him to his feet.

The next instant they shoved him into a leather chair.

The room was still hazy, out of focus. Jay wanted to see the face of the man with the smooth voice so badly it hurt.

"How are you feeling, Jay? I hope you're comfortable,"

Jay moaned.

The smooth voice laughed.

The laugh seemed all so familiar.

Finally, things just clicked. Everything snapped into its rightful place, except nothing was right now that that act had occurred. The man who sat in front of him was none other than his boss. The editor in chief of Superfly Times, Ron Panola.

The son-of-a-bitch had a smug look on his tanned face, and he had a damn bamboo stick in his mouth. Ron had an unhealthy obsession with pandas, and somewhere along the way he picked up chewing bamboo sticks. Jay wanted nothing more in life than to shatter Ron's jaw. However, the rage soon subsided.

Ron clasped his manicured hands into one another. "Let's get down to the bottom line, Jay. I'm not one to waste time. I want the eggs."

Nothing.

That's all Jay could think of when he heard that word. All he could pull up was a nice blank slate of nothingness which he could drown in forever.

"Don't make me ask you again, Jay. Now

where are the fucking eggs? I know you have them," Ron said, furiously.

Jay felt dizzy. His head began to throb.

"I-I don't know . . . what you're . . . talking about."

Ron got up and walked over to Jay and backhanded him across the face.

Jay felt a gash open on the right side of his face below his eye. He stared at Ron's ring, while blood streamed down his cheek.

Ron deeply cherished the 30 karat gold ring. He paraded it in front of others as if it mattered more than his wife. And everyone suspected it did.

Ron quickly wiped the blood off the ring. He looked up and spoke. "I'm not one for games, Jay. You know this. Want to know why? Because this fine couple was hired to keep me in the know about you."

Jay managed to spit out a word. "Why?"

"Well, I don't like you. Surprise. Surprise. Those pandas and the balloons. That happened on purpose, but somehow you lived, you survived. You are a survivor. I'll give you that. But that's beside the point. These two," Ron gestured, "I hired them to kill you. Don't judge them by their looks. They are the best assassins money can buy, believe it or not."

Ron paused and dusted off his shoes made from an extinct breed of panda bear.

Finally, it hit Jay hard and heavy like the blow he received to his face. The eggs. The eggs were special, native to Apeiron. He had to protect them at all costs.

"Look, I'm going to be real with you. You're going to die. By the looks of it, you already are on your way down that path. Mr. and Mrs. Hayes enjoy their job, but none of us have the patience or time to wait for you to stammer and stutter. Just give us the eggs. Then all of us can be on our merry way."

Jay reached into his pockets. His hands came out warm and sticky holding nothing but eggshells. There was nothing but goo down there, a whole bunch of egg yolk.

As Ron noticed Jay's hands, he ran his fingers through his jet black hair. He took a deep breath in an attempt to control his anger.

"Jay, how did those eggs break?"

"I . . . have no idea. My pockets were stuffed full of them but somewhere along the way they were somehow . . . crushed."

"So you don't have what I want. You amount to nothing. The only thing that has kept you alive is sheer luck and those eggs. Now it seems your luck has run out. Dispose of him."

Jay watched as Mr. and Mrs. Hayes slowly got up. Mrs. Hayes reached into her back pocket and pulled out a ginsu knife.

"Time to cut away some of that excess fat."

Jay felt weak, weaker than he had ever been. They probably drugged him earlier. Put some type of junk in his system. He thought about all this while trying to formulate a plan.

There was a loud bang against the door. Then another. The hinges began to strain. It wasn't going to be long before the door broke down.

Mr. and Mrs. Hayes looked backward at the door. Ron fixed his attention on the door as well, his forehead creased in worry.

"What the hell is going on?" Ron yelled in anger.

Jay saw his chance. He knew he had to take it. He wasn't sure how long his window of opportunity was going to last. *It's now or never*, he thought grimly.

Jay lunged at Mrs. Hayes, one hand reaching out for the knife, the other swinging at her old wrinkled face. She cried out in pain and shock as his fist connected with her nose. She dropped the knife, it clanged against the floor.

Mr. Hayes turned around—his face full of worry. He looked at his wife and back at the knife, not sure what was more important.

The kicks against the door continued.

Jay made the decision for him. He kicked the old man hard and swift in the ankle. The old man fell across his wife.

The door began to buckle inward.

Ron was sweating now, trying to keep cool, calm, and collected as he fumbled with his keys, searching for the right one. "Got to get my gun," he said under his breath. The keys kept sliding out of his grip; nothing was going according to plan.

Jay started toward his boss, blood dripping down his hands and face.

The door gave way, slamming against the wall.

Eric floated inside toting a semi-automatic

hand gun.

"Everybody put your hands up, and shut your fucking mouths."

Eric was covered in blood. The clothes over his slabs of meat were in tatters. He looked like he just came back from war, and he was on the winning side.

"Glad to see you, Eric," Jay said.

"You too."

Mr. and Mrs. Hayes laid ontop of each other trembling in fear. Ron had his hands in the air looking at both Eric and Jay as if they were death covered in flesh.

"What should we do with them?" Eric asked.

"To tell you the truth I haven't really thought about that. Any ideas, suggestions?" Jay asked.

"Yeah, I have one." Eric grinned. He cocked his semi-automatic and pulled the trigger. A hail of bullets ripped through Ron and his cherry oak desk.

Ron flailed his arms around like a grotesque puppet having its strings pulled haphazardly. Finally, he stopped moving and slumped across his desk, dead.

Mr. and Mrs. Hayes scrambled towards the door, but Eric cocked back his gun again and shot the old man in the temple and the old woman in the chest. They fell to the ground in a bloody embrace.

The sound of gunshots continued ringing inside Jay's ears.

"What do you give my performance out of

10? 10 being the highest and one being the lowest?" Eric asked.

"I don't know, maybe nine and a half," Jay said.

"Why not a whole ten?"

"You were a little sloppy, and you took too damn long getting here."

"Well I guess it wasn't perfect. But hey, you win some you lose some."

"I guess so."

"Let's leave."

"What about all these bodies?"

"Don't worry about it. In life there's death, and in death there's life."

As they were leaving, Jay looked behind him at the bodies. Leaves began to push their way out of Mr. Hayes' mouth. Jay could barely believe it. Flowers began to blossom out of Mrs. Hayes' eye sockets. The fresh scent of lilies replaced Ron's overwhelming cologne.

38

Jay sat in his apartment, appreciating the softness of his bed. It felt great to be home. He let out a breath of relief and rolled onto his side.

Something fell on the ground barely making a sound.

"What the hell?" Jay said.

Don't even bother, he thought. *It's probably just a pillow.* He closed his eyes and enjoyed the serenity of darkness for a moment before curiosity began to gnaw away at his insides.

He sat up; his muscles popping loudly, and looked at what fell to the floor. An egg was laying right next to a dirty sock.

The egg began to crack.

ABOUT THE AUTHOR

Grant Wamack is a weird fiction writer, rapper, traditional artist, and dreamer. Also, he's the author of A Lightbulb's Lament. During the day, the Navy employs him as a Mass Communication Specialist, in other words a super journalist.

Proof

Made in the USA
Charleston, SC
02 February 2013